THE HARDY BOYS

BOYS

UNDERCOVER BROTHERS®

#17 **Murder at the Mall**

FRANKLIN W. DIXON

Aladdin Paperbacks
New York   London   Toronto   Sydney

🦅 ALADDIN PAPERBACKS
An imprint of Simon & Schuster Children's Publishing Division
1230 Avenue of the Americas, New York, NY 10020
Copyright © 2007 by Simon & Schuster, Inc.
All rights reserved, including the right of reproduction in whole or in part in any form.
THE HARDY BOYS MYSTERY STORIES and HARDY BOYS UNDER-COVER BROTHERS are registered trademarks of Simon & Schuster, Inc.
ALADDIN PAPERBACKS and related logo are registered trademarks of Simon & Schuster, Inc.
Designed by Lisa Vega
The text of this book was set in Aldine 401 BT.
Manufactured in the United States of America
First Aladdin Paperbacks edition July 2007
10 9 8 7 6 5 4 3 2 1
Library of Congress Control Number 2007926412
ISBN-13: 978-1-4169-3930-6
ISBN-10: 1-4169-3930-X

Retail can be deadly!

Adriana showed me around the store for about fifteen minutes. By the time closing time rolled around, the rain had let up, and the sky was getting a little brighter.

She got out her keys, and we stepped out onto the promenade so she could lock up. I was kind of hoping she'd let me walk her to her car. That way, I could get to know her better—and question her some more about the case, of course.

As I waited, I heard a cracking noise coming from above my head—a noise that sounded like . . .

I looked up, just in time to see a huge pane of glass separate from the ceiling and come hurtling down, headed right for us!

THE HARDY BOYS

UNDERCOVER BROTHERS®

Available from Simon & Schuster

TABLE OF CONTENTS

1.

Hard-Boiled Hardys

My skin was burning!

Every breath was like sucking fire straight into my lungs. I pounded on the door, but it was locked from the outside.

Now, I love a good sauna—*most* of the time. But *180 degrees*? Give me a break!

"Any great ideas?" I asked my brother Frank—not because he's a year older than I am, but because he has a long history of thinking us out of trouble.

We'd been on the trail of a notorious people trafficker—a really bad, really rich guy. This sleazebag happened to belong to the very exclusive Moscow Health and Fitness Center—that's Moscow, as in *Russia*.

Working with ATAC (American Teens Against Crime) in partnership with Interpol, Frank and I had followed Mr. Bigski all the way across the Atlantic Ocean and right into this sauna that was about to broil us alive.

Since this particular bad guy had made a specialty of smuggling *teenagers*, Interpol decided that it had to *be* teenagers—Frank and me, disguised as bait—who would track this bad boy down.

Well, we'd tracked him down, all right—straight into this sauna. The only problem was, he'd been onto us—maybe from the very start—and now Frank and I were the ones who were cornered!

When our mark got up and left the sauna, we waited a minute or two, like any good investigator who's tailing a suspect. Only then did we try to follow him. That's when the door refused to budge, and we realized he'd locked us in!

A quick check of the thermostat showed he'd jimmied that, too—the control lever was gone. While 180 degrees Fahrenheit isn't technically *boiling*, it was plenty close enough to finish us off.

I wondered where the pool boy had gone off to. Mr. Bigski must've paid him a handsome tip to get lost, I figured.

"Okay, big brother," I said, folding my arms and sitting back on the redwood bench as the waves of heat rose all around us. "*Now* what do we do?"

"First, I would like to point out," Frank stated, "that it was *your* idea to trail this guy to the health club. Not mine."

"This is no time to argue," I said. He was right, though. It *was* my idea. "Come on, Frank, you know you're the brains of this outfit."

"Flattery will get you nowhere," he said. "Even if it's true."

"I can't even *think* in this heat."

"Well, if you'll just stop *talking* for a minute, I'll take a stab at it." He sighed and lowered his head into his hands.

The heat kept radiating from the lava rocks, hitting me in little waves . . . *thwap* . . . *thwap* . . . *thwap* . . .

If it got any hotter in here, I was definitely going to pass out.

"Don't take too long about it, Frank."

Right on cue, he cried, "I have an idea! Got any metal on you?"

"*Metal?* Frank, we're in our bathing suits!"

"Your chain, man."

"This? This is gold, dude—twenty-four carats!"

"Joe, we haven't got time to fool around here."

It hurt me, but I took off the chain and handed it to him. Then I leaned back on the bench and closed my eyes. I was on the edge of fading out, and I had to keep biting my lip just to stay awake.

Frank grabbed a towel someone had left behind on the bench and wrapped it around his hand to protect it. Then he reached into the pile of steaming lava rocks, jamming the chain deep into the sauna's power source.

There was a sudden spark, and a loud *POP!* In an instant, all the lights went out, and we were in total darkness.

"Frank?" I gasped, fully awake now. "Are you okay?"

I sure hoped he hadn't electrocuted himself trying to save us!

"I . . . I think so," he said in a shaky voice. "I did get shocked pretty good. . . ."

"That was a stupid, *stupid* thing to do, Frank."

"I didn't see much choice, Joe. Either the heat got short-circuited, or we did. It ought to start cooling off in here pretty soon."

"Aw, our brains'll be boiled by then! And meanwhile, we're still locked in."

"You think so? Try the door."

"What?"

"Just try it."

I did—and guess what? *It opened.*

Man, that Frank is smart! How did he know

4

that the lock on the sauna door was hooked up to an electronic release?

"I've gotta hand it to you, Frank," I told him. "In this heat, I couldn't even have thought of my own name, let alone an idea like that."

"Ah, it's nothing."

"Sure you're all right?"

"Nope. Now could we please get moving?"

A faint glow from the club's emergency lighting system filtered in. It pierced the steam that rose from the whirlpool and filled the entire pool enclosure.

In the dim light, I turned and saw Frank—and jumped backward in shock!

His hair was sticking straight up. The ends looked a little charred, and so did his eyebrows—but otherwise, he was definitely alive. His eyes were opened wider than I'd ever seen them. The dry towel that had protected him was charred and smoking as he unwound it from his hand and dropped it on the floor.

"Come on," he said, brushing past me. "Let's get out of here—we've got to catch that guy before he gets away!"

"You think he's still hanging around?" I asked as we entered the shower room. "I doubt it. If I were him, I'd be *long* gone."

But I was wrong. *Again.* Because suddenly the door to one of the shower stalls banged open behind me.

Instinctively, I ducked—and a good thing, too. The gunshot missed my head by inches, ricocheting off the wall and sending pieces of tile flying everywhere.

I went into a roll and buckled the guy's knees. He let out a yelp and went down in a heap, just in time for Frank to yank away his gun while I pummeled him into total submission.

"That wasn't a very nice thing to do, mister," I told him. "But then, you're not a very nice guy, are you?"

He didn't answer. In fact, I'm not sure he heard me. He looked pretty out of it, thanks to my poor sore fists.

"I'll alert the police," said Frank, stepping outside and pulling out his cell phone. "You okay in here alone with him?"

"I'm fine *now*," I answered.

Getting off the passed-out crook, I stepped into a shower stall and turned on the cold water. I needed to cool off *now*, before I passed out myself.

"Sure *you're* okay, Frank?" I asked. "You look kind of . . . electric."

He ran a hand through his hair, which kept

6

standing straight up anyway. "I'm fine," he insisted. "Never felt better in my life. I'm all . . . tingly!"

His whole body shuddered, and I could swear I saw sparks flying. But charged up or not, he was definitely alive, and that was a big relief.

"Ahhh," I said, letting the cold water of the shower pour all over me, while I kept a wary eye on the motionless Mr. Bigski. "You know, you're right, Frank. I do feel pretty good. And I've never felt *cleaner*, either!"

2.
Reality Bites

Ah yes, it was great to be back in the U.S. of A! Russia's a fascinating place to visit, but not when you're being cooked alive.

Besides, after spending the whole school vacation week out of the country, it was nice to have Sunday to veg out before starting school again the next morning.

And with all of Sunday off, what better way to relax than by hanging out at the food court of the good old East Side Mall with our friends, Chet Morton and his sister Iola?

"Tell me the truth," Iola was saying. "I look like a freakazoid in this uniform, right? Come on, you can be honest. I can take it."

"Okay, you look like a freakazoid," Joe said, eyeing her up and down.

"Ahhh! I can't take it!" Iola blew her hair out of her eyes, then shook her head and groaned. "I'm going to quit this job. Right now."

"Wait," I said, putting a hand on her shoulder to keep her from getting up. "You said you need the work."

"I don't need it *that* bad," she said, looking down at her weird uniform from Phil's Phranks 'n' Phries—the one that made her look like a Phrank with mustard.

Chet put a hand on her shoulder. "Just keep thinking, 'I'm going to Montreal on the class trip. . . . I'm going to Mon—'"

"Okay, okay!" she said, letting out a huge sigh. "I won't quit. But this outfit is just too much. I'm a walking fashion nightmare!"

"Hey, it could be worse," Chet said. "You could be dressed as a taco." He nodded toward Tio's Tacos, whose workers were all wearing taco shell hats.

See, that's the great thing about East Side Mall. It's not like all those new squeaky-clean megamalls that have no character at all.

No, East Side is a dinosaur among malls. Its

9

stores are mostly independents, not chains—and they sell really cool, unusual stuff, too. Maybe that's why it's been a favorite hangout for Bayport's teens since the day it opened, thirty long years ago.

True, the place had seen better days. Everything looked just a little bit shabby, and the crowds weren't what they used to be. Over the past couple of years, some of East Side's biggest and best stores had closed—including that great old one-of-a-kind department store, Raymond's.

Maybe it was because the East Side neighborhood was a little out-of-the-way. Other than the mall, there weren't too many reasons for townies to drive way out here—not yet, anyway. But I remembered reading in the paper that the East Side was going to be Bayport's next hot neighborhood.

"How are *you* going to afford the trip, Chet?" asked Iola.

"Huh?" It was obvious he'd never even thought about it.

"The *trip? Montreal?* You said you were coming, remember?" Iola reminded him. "And our parents aren't paying for it."

"You got that right," Chet said, snorting. "I still haven't paid them back for the repair work on their Chevy."

"The one you backed into the fire hydrant?" Joe asked.

"Is there another?" He sighed sadly. "I guess I'm gonna have to find a job too."

"Phil's still hiring," Iola suggested. "He's *always* hiring."

"No way," said Chet quickly. "I'm not sinking *that* low. There's got to be a better job than that."

"Good luck," she told him. "I looked for two weeks before I gave up and took this one."

"Well, if I get desperate, I'll let you know," said Chet.

"How 'bout you two?" Iola asked me and Joe. "You thinking of coming on the trip? Maybe you ought to get jobs here too."

"Uh . . . yeah, I guess," I responded, giving Joe a look.

"Maybe," said Joe, equally uneasy.

See, the thing is, not many people know about our undercover work for ATAC. Certainly not Iola and Chet—knowing would only put them in danger, and might also mess up one of our missions.

But it's hard to take a job when you might have to quit at any moment to go after some bad guy or other. Same goes for class trips. We must have lost our deposits at least three times.

"You guys ought to consider it," Iola urged. "Working builds character."

We all stared at her uniform, shaking our heads.

"In my case, a *lot* of character," she added.

"You know, I really *should* get a job," Chet said, suddenly getting serious. "I've been working with my personal trainer, and he's not cheap, believe me. I know my mom and dad are happy to pay for it, but I really should start contributing."

"Hey, man—whatever you're paying him, he's worth it," said Joe. "Frank, check out these biceps." He squeezed Chet's arm, and Chet made a muscle so we could all admire the trainer's expensive work.

"I've been bench-pressing over three hundred pounds," Chet bragged.

"Get out!" I said.

"Uh-huh," replied Chet, with a smug smile on his face. "Eat your heart out."

For almost his whole life, Chet had been . . . well, overweight. But something must have snapped, because suddenly he swore off the junk food and started working out with that trainer of his. In just a few months, Chet's stomach went from a hunk of flab to a concrete slab.

"I think I'll take a little stroll around and see who's hiring," he said, flexing his pecs.

"Now?" asked Joe.

"Hey, there's no time like the present," Chet shot back. Wading through the lunchtime crowd, he disappeared from view.

Iola sipped on her chocolate milkshake and said, "You know Phil, my boss? He says this mall's going downhill fast, because of all the kids hanging out."

I glanced around the food court. Sure enough, most of the people at the food court were kids around our age.

"What's wrong with kids hanging out?" Joe asked.

"He says it scares people with real money away."

"I don't get it," said Joe. "What's so scary about kids?"

Iola arched her eyebrows and turned toward the food court entrance, where a group of teens about our age had taken up positions along the low stone wall.

I counted seven of them—five guys and two girls. The guys all had the same buzz cuts, ripped-up T-shirts, and cargo pants. Their shoes had either no laces, or laces that weren't tied. Three of the guys had tattoos on their arms or necks, and two of them had eyebrow rings.

The two girls had about five earrings in each ear,

pierced noses, and ripped jeans. One of them was wearing a tank top that showed a navel ring and a tattoo on her back. The other was wearing an old motorcycle vest, so I couldn't tell what else she'd done to herself.

"See those kids?" Iola said. "They're here all the time—sometimes till closing time. I mean, they're harmless and all, and they mostly just hang out by the emergency stairs. But if you were a little old lady with lots of cash in your wallet and bags of expensive merchandise in your hands, would you want to run into them on your way back to the parking deck?"

"Okay, I get your point," said Joe, frowning.

"Scary or not, kids still have real money to spend," I pointed out. "Their *parents'* money."

"Yeah, but it's not the same thing," Iola argued. "Of course, Phil says it doesn't matter to him, because kids'll eat Phranks 'n' Phries till they barf. But he says a lot of the stores here are on the edge of going out of business. They're even talking about tearing this whole place down and building a new, chichi mall instead."

"Yuck!" Joe said. "Who'd want to come hang out in a place like that?"

"Exactly," said Iola. "Bingo! No teenagers hanging out means more older people with charge cards and expense accounts ringing up big purchases. Of course, it also means the big chains'll move in, and all the little mom-and-pop stores'll disappear."

"That really bites," I said. "This place rules."

"Yeah, well, enjoy it while you can." She sighed, got up, and took her tray to the trash can. "I've gotta get back to work. See you guys later, okay?"

"Sure thing." I waved as she walked away.

"Catch you later," Joe called. Then he looked down and said, "Hey! What the—?"

"What?"

"How'd this get here?" he wondered, lifting up a Silly Meal bag from Burgerama. "This isn't mine."

"It's not?"

"You know I had sushi."

"Let me see that," I said, reaching over and grabbing the bag.

Inside was a kid-size burger and portion of fries—but instead of the little plastic toy, there was a mini-DVD!

"Hey, Joe," I exclaimed, my pulse starting to race as I pulled it out and held it up to show him. "Guess what?"

"Whoa," he said, his eyes widening with excitement as he read the initials on the tape: ATAC.

• • • •

"Hello, boys."

The voice was that of Q, our boss at ATAC. The picture on my computer monitor was familiar—in fact, it was the front entrance of the East Side Mall.

"Sorry to call on you again so soon, but you know how these things are. And this case is close to home, so you won't have to miss school."

"Aw, man," Joe whined. "I was hoping for a trip to Hawaii."

"You're looking at the East Side Mall, of course—a Bayport institution," Q went on. "But what you may not be aware of is that the mall owner, a certain Mr. Arthur Applegate, is considering selling the property. Apparently an offer has been made, by a certain Shangri-La Enterprises, LLC—a nationwide but locally based developer specializing in high-class mega-malls."

The picture changed: Huge, glittering, glass-walled malls, with stores selling merchandise priced in the thousands—diamond jewelry, sculptures, and other stuff no kid would or could ever buy.

"The mayor and city council are in favor of the sale," Q went on, "at least, so far. But there are problems, I'm afraid. Apparently the possibility of a sale has angered certain people. In the past week Mr. Applegate has received no fewer than three e-mailed threats, warning him not to sell to Shangri-La."

We saw the three e-mails projected on the screen. They were basically printouts from computer files, complete with misspellings. The first one was straight to the point: "DON'T SELL TO SHANGRI-LA. Here's why: Shangri-La Enterprises plans to knock down the current mall and build a much larger one. If this happens, it will pave over a precious fourteen-acre wetland!" It was signed STEMM (Save the East Side Marsh and Mall). The Ms in STEMM were interlocked, forming a logo.

"Hmm," I said. "Doesn't sound very threatening to me."

"Me neither," agreed Joe.

But the second e-mail was much darker: "How much are they offering you to sell out endangered species?" It went on to list several rare insects and plants, along with a threatened subspecies of water rat. The e-mail ended: "This sale MUST NOT HAPPEN! You have forty-eight hours to call it off."

The third e-mail was the shortest of the three: "Only twenty-four hours left. STOP THE SALE NOW, or what happens will be your own fault. STEMM."

"In case you're wondering," Q said, "STEMM seems to be a small, relatively new environmental group. They deny sending the e-mails, which were traced to an Internet café in downtown Bayport. We want to find out more about the group—who they are, and what they're planning to do if the sale isn't canceled.

"That's why we want you two to go undercover at the mall. Find yourselves jobs there and get to know everyone with a stake in this case. Your job is to find out who's been sending those e-mails, so we can stop them from going any further."

"Is this weird or what?" Joe said, shaking his head in amazement. "Weren't we just talking about getting jobs at the mall?"

"Yeah, but we weren't really going to *do* it," I pointed out. "I can just see you in one of those Phranks 'n' Phries uniforms. . . ."

"Shut up!" Joe said, punching me lightly on the arm. "There is *no possible way!*"

"Shhh," I told him. "Q's not finished."

"Remember, no one at the mall knows why you're there. Not even Mr. Applegate himself. Good luck, boys—and be careful. This may be nothing, or it may be quite dangerous. Only time will tell. Oh, and speaking of time—as usual, this DVD will self-destruct in three . . . two . . . one . . ."

The screen started flashing rainbow patterns, and a song by Fleshfire blasted out of the speakers.

But Joe and I didn't stick around to hear it. We were already halfway down the stairs, on our way back to the mall.

3.

Dangerous Work

"I feel like we just left here," I shouted over the engine noise as we steered our motorcycles into the East Side Mall's indoor parking deck.

"Dude, we *did* just leave here."

"Oh, yeah—right. Well, it's not exactly a glamorous assignment."

Frank laughed. "You never know. Life's full of surprises."

We parked, locked our helmets onto the bikes, and headed into the mall itself.

"I can't believe this," I said. "I'm about to get an *actual job!*"

"Hey, look at the bright side," said Frank. "You might actually make some money on this case. That'd be a first!"

"Are you kidding? ATAC would never let us keep it."

All monies taken in on ATAC cases go right back into the agency's budget, and both Frank and I knew it. Oh, well—it's not like we're in it for the money, anyway.

"Well, I sure hope we solve this one fast," I said. "I don't want to get stuck slinging Phries for the rest of my life."

"Hey, who says Phil's hiring?"

"Iola says he's *always* hiring, remember?"

"Hmm . . . maybe you ought to try something else before you get that desperate."

"Good idea. Those uniforms are a definite no-go zone."

We were almost to the food court now. "You know, Joe, we should probably split up and get jobs in different parts of the mall. That way we'll be able to see twice as much of what's going on."

"Good idea. But I don't see myself selling jeans or something. The food court's more my speed. Why don't you try getting a job in one of the stores?"

"Okay," he said. "Later. Call me on my cell if you get hired."

"You too."

Frank went on ahead, passing the fountain and

the nearby emergency stairs, while I approached the food court.

There was that same gang of kids, still sitting on the low wall that separated the food court from the promenade. They were busy giving one of the mall's security guards a hard time—or maybe it was the other way around, I couldn't be sure.

"You can't stay here, okay?" the guard was saying.

"Why not?" said the biggest and meanest-looking of the group. "It's a free country."

"It's loitering, that's why not."

I could see why security was not pleased to have these kids hanging around. They weren't exactly good for business. On the other hand, they were right—it *is* a free country, and they weren't blocking the way or hassling anybody, as far as I could see.

Since I was here to investigate threats to the mall, I made a mental note to keep an eye on them, then went on into the food court to get myself a job.

Because East Side was an older mall, its food court wasn't that big a deal—just an ordinary circular area with tables in the center and fast food booths all around the edges.

The nicest thing about it was that the big chains—McDonald's, KFC, and all the rest—were nowhere in sight. Every one of the stores here was an original, one-of-a-kind place, which is really cool when you stop and think about it.

I turned slowly in a circle. Hot Wired Coffee . . . Tio's Tacos . . . Wok Around the Clock . . . Pizza My Mind . . . Mount Sushi . . . Cookie Crumbles . . . Burgerama . . . Phil's Phranks 'n' Phries . . .

I waved to Iola, and she waved a Phrank back at me before handing it to a customer. Wow, Phil's sure was doing a brisk business—there had to be at least a dozen customers on each of his three lines!

In fact, *most* of the booths were doing a brisk business.

Hmm. Not good.

See, I was looking for a place that had *no* customers—or at least, as few as possible. I couldn't really look out for trouble at the mall if I was busy serving people, could I?

I resumed my scan of the food court. Mount Sushi . . . The Big Chill . . . hey, wait a minute— wasn't that Chet behind the counter, scooping a heap of Death by Chocolate into a gigantic sugar cone?

That stupid, cone-shaped hat—it looked like a chocolate dunce cap—kind of hid those familiar chipmunk cheeks, but it was him all right!

"Hey, Chet!"

"Yo!" He nodded and grinned as I came up to the counter and slapped him five.

"*Ice cream*, Chet?"

"Why not?"

I gave him a look.

"Don't worry, Joe—there's no chance I'll start gorging on this stuff. I'm not going to go and ruin my entire super-fitness program—not after all the work I've done these past few months!"

"You're amazing, dude," I said. "If it was me, no way could I resist."

"Strong like bull," Chet grunted, making a huge muscle for me. And I mean *huge*.

"Dude, I've got to talk with your trainer and see if he's got time to work with me!"

"He's the best. But I don't know if you're tough enough to hang with it, Joe."

"*What?*"

Chet laughed. "Just messing with you," he said. "Yeah, sure, I'll ask him."

"Hey! How 'bout serving some customers?" Chet's boss snapped at him.

"Sure thing, Ernesto," Chet said, and got back to work.

"And quit giving out such huge portions!"

Ernesto added in a whisper that was loud enough for everyone to hear. "I'm in this to make money, not to make people happy!"

Sheesh, I thought. *I'd sure hate to work for a boss like that!*

Right next to the Big Chill was a stand called Healthy Wraps. And guess what? There wasn't a soul waiting on line. *Not one person.*

"Hi," I said to the guy leaning over the counter with his chin in his hands. "How's it going?"

He glanced left and right, looking bored and defeated. "How's it look?"

"Uh, not too great, I'd say."

He nodded, sighing. "It's . . . a little slow at the moment."

"Sorry to hear that."

He heaved a heavy sigh. "I just opened up last week, and it's taking a while to catch on. A lot longer than I thought, to tell you the truth."

"Really? Why do you think that is?"

"It's not the food, I can tell you that!" he said, leaning forward over the counter. "People would love my wraps, if they'd only try them."

"I guess this is a stupid question, but . . . you wouldn't be hiring, would you?"

"*Hiring?* Are you *crazy*? You think I need help with all these millions of customers?"

"Well, maybe if you had someone *younger* behind the counter—you know, someone with a little 'youth appeal,' it might draw more of the young crowd."

"Look," he told me, "you seem like a nice kid. Honestly? I'd love to hire you. Nothing would give me more pleasure than to get out of here every day by four in the afternoon. I'm sick of sitting here all by myself, waiting for business to pick up. It's frustrating, you know? But I can't afford to hire anybody. I'm losing money as it is."

That's when I brought out my ace in the hole. "Well," I said, "how about I start as a volunteer? Just until business picks up, of course."

His eyebrows rose, and he looked me up and down in surprise. "You would do that?"

"For a while, yeah. A week, say."

"Mind if I ask why?"

Okay, now I had to think quick. I mean, I couldn't tell him the *real* reason—that I wanted to work in a place where I could pursue the case of the threatening e-mails, undisturbed by annoying customers.

"Because I'm sure I can get kids to try your delicious Healthy Wraps, that's why!" I don't know where those words came from—they just popped out of my mouth, like toast from a toaster.

He frowned. "How do you know they're so delicious? You haven't even tried one!"

"Well . . . let me try one now! If I like it, and think I can sell it, I'll work for you for free for a week. What do you say?"

He squinted hard at me. I guess he was trying to figure out whether I was trying to put one over on him, or if I was just plain stupid. "What's your name, kid?"

"Joe," I said, sticking out my hand. "Joe Hardy."

He shook it. "You drive a hard bargain, Joe. I'm Clem Bartlett—and you're hired!"

"Great!"

"But right now, the dinner rush is about to start, and even *this* place is gonna get a customer or two. So why don't you come back around closing time? You can have yourself a free Healthy Wrap, and if you still want the job, I'll show you everything you need to know."

"See you at closing time, then," I said, giving him a little wave and backing away.

"*Yes!*" I whispered as I headed over to Phil's Phranks 'n' Phries. It had taken me all of ten minutes to land a job!

Okay, it was for no pay—at least for a week, by which time I was sure the case would be solved and I could quit. But more importantly, I had a *job*—and I was *sure* Frank was still unemployed. Ha! Take that, big brother.

"How's it going, Iola?" I asked as I sidled up to the counter, ignoring the huge line of customers in front of her.

Phil's Phranks 'n' Phries was the busiest place in the whole food court. Iola had her hands full, for sure. She was working like a demon. So were her two coworkers—kids I knew from Bayport High.

As for the boss himself, Phil was sitting in one corner, watching an international soccer match on TV, paying no attention to what was going on around him.

"He's kind of weird," Iola told me. "A total soccer freak. If there's a match on, I could walk away and come back in half an hour, and he'd never notice."

"Hey, I've gotta book," I said. "But I'm going to be working over at Healthy Wraps."

"*What?*"

"No lie."

"I can't believe he really needs help!"

I cleared my throat. "I think he's just too depressed to want to hang around a sinking ship." No need to mention my starting salary, I figured.

Well, it was back to real business for me.

Closing time at the East Side Mall was eight p.m. on Sundays. Which meant I had almost an hour to snoop around.

Halfway down the promenade, I passed a narrow corridor marked PRIVATE: MALL OFFICES. AUTHORIZED PERSONNEL ONLY.

Well, *that* got my attention. I checked to make sure no one was looking, then ducked down the little hallway.

There were a couple of unmarked doors on either side. One of them was open—just a crack—and I could hear muffled voices coming from the other side.

They seemed to be arguing. That made me even more curious, so I edged closer to the door, leaned against the wall, and tried to look casual in case anyone spotted me lurking there.

I could hear the raised voices of the two men inside the office. Daring to peek, I recognized one of them from his picture on the DVD from ATAC. He was the mall's owner, Arthur Applegate. He was old—short and fat, with a thin gray mustache and long hair combed back over his bald spot. His suit had grease stains on it, and his desk was a mess of papers and fast food containers.

The other guy didn't look at all familiar. He was younger—maybe forty—thin, with glasses and an expensive gray suit. He had a disgusted look on his face. I wasn't sure if it was because of the messy office or something else.

"I know you're attached to this place," he said to Mr. Applegate, "but you've got to realize, change can't be stopped. The East Side Mall is going to come down, with your help or without it."

"Are you threatening me, Mr. Meister?" Mr. Applegate said, rising from his chair and leaning over his desk toward the other man. "Wait, let me turn on my tape recorder. I'm sure the city council will be interested to hear any threats you have to make on behalf of Shangri-La Enterprises."

I knew that name too—it was the name of the megacorporation that wanted to buy the mall!

"I'm not threatening anything," said Meister. "I would never do that, sir. And please, call me Bob."

"What for?" Mr. Applegate retorted. "So we can be buddy-pals?"

Meister smiled. "Look, I may be a lawyer, but I'm also a human being," he said.

Mr. Applegate laughed. "Right. Sure. You're more shark than human, if you ask me."

"Mr. Applegate," continued the lawyer, "let's stay calm, shall we? Shangri-La is simply looking to buy an attractive property for development. And let me remind you that we're offering a handsome payment—enough for you to buy a luxurious retirement estate for yourself, someplace where it's warm even in winter."

"Who says I want to retire?" shouted Applegate.

Meister shrugged. "Sometimes an offer comes along that you just can't refuse. And you are in your seventies, are you not? I don't mean to be rude, but lots of people retire younger than that."

Applegate sighed. "Look, Mr. Meister. I'm an old man, it's true. But I have my reasons not to sell."

"And those would be?"

"Those would be my business, not anyone else's," said Applegate, annoyed again.

"I see," said Meister, flashing a weary smile. "Well, then, Mr. Applegate, I wish you luck keeping this place open. I'm afraid you may need it."

"Threatening me again?" Applegate roared, pounding the desk.

"I wouldn't *dream* of it," replied Meister, adjusting his glasses. "But I can see how things are here. Things are going downhill fast."

"What's that supposed to mean?"

"I see the sort of people this place attracts," Meister said, wrinkling his nose in disgust. "Vagrants. Teenage gang members. Vandals."

31

"We don't have any more trouble here than at any other mall," Applegate insisted.

"Not yet, perhaps," said Meister. "But I can see which way the wind is blowing. You're going to need some serious security around here—and you know how expensive that is."

"I don't like the idea of keeping young people away," stated Applegate, coming around the side of his desk.

I ducked so neither he nor Meister would see me as they turned in my direction. "Kids need a safe place to hang around. Malls should be a community place, not some sterile thing where only rich people can afford to shop!"

"When Shangri-La builds a mall," Meister said, "the stores are spectacular, and the customers have real money to spend. Mr. Applegate, think for a moment before you back out of this deal. Think of the future of Bayport, the city you love. The East Side could be a true destination. People would come here for shopping, movies, restaurants. That awful marsh out there will be a massive, shiny-new parking deck, and those juvenile delinquents you love so much will be nowhere in sight. Good riddance, I say. Let them find another place to trash."

"They're not juvenile delinquents!" Applegate

declared. "I've known some of those kids' parents since *they* were kids."

"Have it your way, Mr. Applegate," said Meister.

I could hear him backing up toward me, and I knew I should book—but I needed to hear what else he had to say!

"I'll bet some of those kids are in with those wacky enviro-nuts from STEMM," said Meister.

"That's ridiculous," Applegate replied, snorting. "And who says they're wacky? They just want to save the marsh, that's all."

"Mmm, yes—save the endangered mosquitoes, I suppose . . . but a little birdie told me they were wacky enough to threaten you—which is something neither I nor Shangri-La would ever do."

"You're smooth, Meister," said Mr. Applegate.

Meister smiled and nodded his head. "Well, I've got to be going, Mr. A. Think it over for a while—but don't take too long. Our offer is time-sensitive. Here's my card in case you want to chat. That number is my direct line."

I heard the sound of paper ripping. Once . . . twice . . . three times.

"I'm sorry you feel that way, Mr. Applegate," said Meister. "You'll see, someday you'll come begging us on your hands and knees to buy you out. But when you do, you'll have to take our rock-bottom offer—and it will be *rock bottom*, I assure you."

He cleared his throat, and I heard something that sounded like fumbling with the locks on a briefcase.

I had to risk taking another look. I leaned in and saw Meister take out a small leather case. From it he removed another business card.

"Let's try this again," he said. With his left hand, he wrote something on the card and left it on Applegate's desk. "That's my direct line. Please don't hesitate to call if you change your mind." He offered his hand, but Applegate didn't shake it.

"Don't hold your breath," Applegate growled. "I won't be calling."

And just then, wouldn't you know it, my stupid cell phone went off!

AAAHH!

Why hadn't I shut it off the minute I came down this hallway? You know, sometimes I can be a total space cadet.

Before I could sprint back down the hallway to the promenade, Meister threw open the door and pinned me against the opposite wall.

"Hey!" he snarled. "What are you doing here? This is a private area!"

"Oh—s-sorry!" I stammered. "I must've gotten confused . . . by the sign . . ."

Lame, lame, lame!

Meister scowled, giving me the once-over as he

SUSPECT PROFILE

Name: Bob Meister, Esq.

Hometown: Bayport

Physical description: Age 40, 5' 9", 150 lbs., pale complexion, spectacles, close-cropped dark hair, sickly smile.

Occupation: Lawyer for Shangri-La Enterprises.

Background: Decided to study law so he could punish bad people. Trouble was, he thinks all people are bad and deserve punishment. Sued his parents while still in law school. Never married. No children (and a good thing, too!).

Suspicious behavior: Threatening the mall's owner (or was it just a friendly warning?).

Suspected of: Using hardball tactics to get Applegate to sell the East Side Mall—but are those tactics strictly legal?

Possible motives: Money, money, money.

---

let me go. I could tell he didn't believe a word I said. "Don't let it happen again, punk."

"N-no, sir!" I said, backing away, then turning and making for the promenade, going as fast as I could without running.

I felt a chill go through me, and it stayed with me as I walked back toward the food court.

That guy Meister was a chilly character, all right. And now I'd gone and made an enemy of him.

The question was, how dangerous an enemy was he?

4.
Help Wanted?

After half an hour of looking for work and getting nowhere, I was beginning to think maybe it was *me*. Why was nobody around here hiring?

Iola had a job. Chet had a job. I wondered if Joe was having a hard time too. I'd already tried every clothing and shoe store, as well as the pet store, the video game store, the hat store, the sunglasses store—and got no results. Toy stores, zilch. Bookstores? Nada.

"Good thing you're an ATAC agent and don't need to look for a real-life job," I told myself, sitting on the marble edge of the fountain. I needed a short "get-it-together" break before I went back to the hunt.

"Hey, you!" a heavily accented, gruff voice

37

shouted. "No sitting there! Don' you see sign?"

"Me?" I asked, pointing to myself.

The guy yelling at me was not a security guard. He was wearing dark green overalls with an EAST SIDE MALL patch sewed to the chest and the name OSKAR embroidered underneath.

He was kind of old to be a janitor—tall, hulking, and bald except for a fringe of wild, curly gray hair. It grew out of his ears too. Flakes of white dandruff decorated his shoulders, and a faint smell of unwashed clothes wafted in my direction.

"Yeah, you," he said. "You want sit, find bench."

He was leaning on something that looked like a push broom, except that the bottom was not a broom, but metal mesh. "What's that you've got there?" I asked, curious.

"This? For fishing," he said, indicating the fountain. "Get coins from pool, give to charity."

"Ah, I see."

"Okay? You don't sit here no more."

"No, I get it. Thanks, Oskar."

He frowned. "I know you from somewhere?"

I pointed to the name on his chest. "My name's Frank," I said. "Frank Hardy."

"Yeah? So what?"

"I'm . . . uh, I'm looking for work here at the mall. You know of anyone who's hiring?"

38

"You want my job?" he asked, offering me the coin-fisher. Then he laughed, showing broken, blackened teeth. "Listen, this mall *finished*. *Kaput*. Rich millionaire gonna buy, tear down, make new one. Then maybe young kid like you find good job in nice store. Not like now."

He looked over at the group of kids Iola'd pointed out before. They'd moved on from the wall by the food court and were now hanging out by the emergency stairs.

"You see kids over there?" he grumbled. "They keep nice people away. Somebody gots to get rid of them."

"It must be tough for you," I said, figuring maybe Oskar might know a thing or two about what went on here at the East Side Mall, and that it would be a good thing to get him talking about it. "Do those kids give you a hard time?"

"Not so much—but make dirty, make loud noises, scare customers," he replied. "Listen, I night watchman here too. After close, I gotta chase those kids away. They no want go home."

"Hmm. Maybe their homes aren't such fun places to go back to."

He shrugged. "So what? No come here, make frighten older people."

I could see that I wasn't going to convince

him to cut those kids a break. So I stopped trying and changed the subject. "Oskar, how many coins do people throw in here, anyway?" I asked, nodding toward the fountain and the pool that surrounded it.

"A lot coins! Very many!" he said, suddenly angry. "And you see what happen? Look!" He gestured toward the pool, which had very few coins in it.

"What do you mean?" I asked. "Didn't you just collect them?"

"No! I come collect, but somebody steal coins before me! They take this first, from broom closet," he said, shaking his mesh broom at me. "I find, you know where? Bottom of water!"

He was still staring at the kids by the stairs, and I could tell he suspected them of the evil deed. But I had to wonder—if they *had* done it, would they still be hanging around with all those coins in their pockets, waiting to get caught?

"I call security guy, but he think *I* steal!" Oskar ranted, spit and foam flying out of his mouth. "Nobody like immigrant, but I not steal! Not like most people."

"I'm sure you didn't, Oskar," I said. "Um, when exactly did you notice the coins had been taken?"

"Just now. Hey, what your name again?"

"Frank. Frank Hardy."

"Frank, why you ask so much question, Frank? You some kinda cop or something?"

Oops. It was time for me to back off, before I blew my cover to smithereens.

"Nah, I was just curious, that's all."

"Lots people around this place up to no good," said Oskar. "Not just young people—*lots* people. I see everything." He tapped his forehead, nodding slowly.

"Oh, yeah? Like who?"

His eyes narrowed, and he looked me up and down suspiciously. "Never mind who," he said. Then he put his fingers to his lips and pretended to lock them with a key.

So I was right about Oskar—he probably knew more about what was going on around here than anyone else.

But now was not the time to pump him for information. That would have to wait for when he wasn't in such a bad mood.

"You're right," I said, patting him on the arm. "It's none of my business. Well, nice meeting you, Oskar. See you around."

He watched me go, muttering something to himself.

Yes, I thought, there was lots more to old Oskar

than met the eye. I made a mental note to check up on him again, *real soon*.

Well, at least the evening hadn't been a *total* waste. I decided to give Joe a call and see how he was making out, so I took out my cell and backed into the doorway of a store, to get out of the flow of human traffic on the promenade.

Joe didn't pick up, and I didn't feel like leaving a message. I had just hung up when somebody tapped me lightly on the shoulder. I turned to see a girl looking at me, smiling.

"Can I help you?" she asked.

"Um, why do you ask? Do I look lost?"

"No, but you're standing here in the store, so . . ."

I suddenly realized that while dialing, I must have stepped back into the actual store—In the Groove, it was called. It offered lava lamps, incense burners, disco balls, black lights, weird T-shirts, posters, and lots of other novelty items.

"Oh, I get it," I said. "You *work* here."

"Yup. Were you looking for something special?"

"Oh—no! I was just . . . um, making a phone call."

"Oh . . . I see. So, where's your phone?"

"In my pocket."

42

SUSPECT PROFILE

Name: Oskar Zemeckis

Hometown: Zagreb, Croatia

Physical description: Age 65, 6' 2", 220 lbs. Has a problem with cleanliness and grooming. Narrow, beady, suspicious eyes. Thinks the worst of everybody—maybe because he knows himself too well?

Occupation: Janitor/night watchman for East Side Mall

Background: Came over from Eastern Europe while it was still behind the Iron Curtain. Arrived uneducated and penniless. Has had a hard life here in America. Who knows what kind of stuff (legal and illegal) he's had to do to get by in a foreign land?

Suspicious behavior: Talking to himself, blaming others for the disappearance of coins he was responsible for collecting and turning over for charity.

Suspected of: Taking the coins and blaming it on those lazy American kids. If he did that, what else is he capable of?

Possible motives: Hey, life is hard. For a guy as nasty as Oskar, it's easy to justify taking a little extra money here and there, especially if people are literally throwing it away.

"Aren't you going to need it? To make a call, I mean?"

"No—um, I tried to call my brother, but he didn't pick up."

"Ah. Well, let me know if I can help you with anything."

"Wait!" I said.

"Yes?"

First of all, let me say straight up, I am *so* not good at talking to girls. Especially if they're staring right at me with huge, gorgeous brown eyes, like this one was.

"You don't go to Bayport High, do you?" I asked.

"No, I live out in East Bay."

"My name's Frank."

"Adriana," she said, shaking my hand with her fingertips. "Nice to meet you, Frank."

"You, um, know if they're looking for help here?"

"Why, you want a job?"

"Uh, yeah. Part-time. You know."

"Yeah—most jobs here are part-time."

"Yeah. Of course."

For some reason, I always turn into a complete geek whenever I'm face-to-face with a girl I really *like*.

"You'd have to ask Steph. She's my boss."

"Steph?"

"Stephanie Flowers. She's around here somewhere—probably back in the stockroom. Let me check."

A minute later Adriana came back, trailed by what I can only describe as someone straight out of the sixties. "Steph," as Adriana called her, was pretty much a retro-hippie—from her long, braided hair to her fringed suede vest. The vest, by the way, was covered with more than a dozen buttons, most of which were about saving the environment.

In fact, one of them said STEMM—with the two Ms linked. I remembered that was the environmental group Q had told us about—the one that supposedly sent the threatening e-mails to Applegate.

Steph stared me up and down. "Have you got references?"

"Uh . . ."

"No references, huh?" She frowned and folded her arms. "Well, I guess I could give you a shot. Adriana seems to like you, and she's got good instincts. And to be honest with you, I could use the help."

I looked inside the store. There were only two customers, standing at the cash register as Adriana rang up their purchases. "Really?" I said. "It doesn't look that busy. . . ."

"True, but weekday afternoons, a lot of kids come in here. Besides, I've got other things going on right now, and I can't be stuck here all afternoon and evening. So if you want a job, like I said, I'll give you a try."

"Great!" I shook her hand, which had about ten rings on it. "Thanks. When can I start?"

Steph looked at her watch. "Well, it's almost closing time, so how about you come back tomorrow?"

"Is four o'clock okay? I've got school. . . ."

"Great. See you at four . . . Frank, is it?"

"Yes, ma'am. Frank Hardy."

"Don't call me ma'am—call me Steph. Everyone else does."

We shook hands again. Steph stepped out onto the promenade and looked up at the roof of the mall. It tilted upward on one side, which was almost entirely made up of glass skylights held together by a thin metal frame. Usually the glass let a lot of light through. At the moment, though, the sky was pretty dark.

"It's going to pour any minute," said Steph. "I'm outta here. Adriana, will you lock up?"

"Sure thing."

"Uh, Steph?" I said. "I couldn't help noticing your buttons."

46

"Oh, these? Yeah, I'm pretty 'out there,' I know."

"What does that one mean?" I asked, pointing to the STEMM button.

"Ah—it means Save the East Side Marsh and Mall. I'm the president," she told me. "We aim to keep this place just as it is—safe for animals and people."

"You know," I said, taking a chance, "I heard something about e-mails to the owner of this mall, warning him not to sell. Weren't they supposed to have come from STEMM?"

Steph stared at me, her expression as dark as the sky overhead. "Where'd you hear that?"

"I don't remember," I lied. "But is it true?"

"Definitely not! That rumor is just a bunch of baloney, spread by the forces of evil."

The forces of evil?

Right on cue, there was a tremendous clap of thunder, and rain started pouring down on the roof, pattering loudly on the glass skylights.

"Somebody else is signing our name to those messages!" Steph insisted.

"Why would they do that?" I asked.

"To make us look bad, of course! And so that the city council and the mayor will approve the sale of the mall."

SUSPECT PROFILE

Name: Stephanie "Steph" Flowers

Hometown: Bayport

Physical description: Age 30, 5' 4", 120 lbs. Looks and dresses like a hippie from the sixties. Tie-dye and paisley to the max.

Occupation: Manager of In the Groove, one of the East Side Mall's signature stores, catering to young people.

Background: Grew up in Bayport and became a dedicated environmentalist in college, where she stayed for seven years. Has been in retail ever since she got divorced from her husband, who was her high school sweetheart. No children, but cares deeply about all children and other living things.

Suspicious behavior: She's the president of STEMM, the group implicated in the threatening e-mails to Applegate.

Suspected of: Making threats against the mall and its owner, trying to prevent the mall's sale. Potentially planning violent acts if their demands aren't met.

Possible motives: Saving the mall and its surrounding marsh (and all the cute little animals and plants that live there).

"But aren't they already in favor of the sale?" I asked.

Uh-oh. Now I'd gone and made Steph mad. Her face got all red, and she wagged her finger in my face. "If this place gets sold to Shangri-La, you know what comes next?"

"Uh, no. What?"

"I'll *tell* you what comes next—stores like this one will disappear from the new mall, and so will the kind of customers it draws. Teenagers and young adults will be just as endangered around here as the creatures who live in the marsh outside! Well, let me tell you something, Frank—*that is never going to happen.*"

Steph sure seemed committed to her cause. I had to wonder if, in spite of what she said, she really could be trusted to stay nonviolent if things came to a crisis. From the fiery look in her eyes, and the hot tone of her voice, I got the impression that she had a pretty explosive temper.

After Steph had gone, Adriana said, "She gets a little worked up sometimes, but she's really pretty nice. You'll see."

Yeah, I thought. *Pretty nice, if you're on her good side.*

Adriana showed me around the store for about

49

fifteen minutes. By the time closing time rolled around, the rain had let up, and the sky was getting a little brighter.

She got out her keys, and we stepped out onto the promenade so she could lock up. I was kind of hoping she'd let me walk her to her car. That way, I could get to know her better—and question her some more about the case, of course.

As I waited, I heard a cracking noise coming from above my head—a noise that sounded like . . .

I looked up, just in time to see a huge pane of glass separate from the ceiling and come hurtling down, headed right for us!

JOE

5.
Shattered Illusions

I was almost all the way back to the food court for my appointment at Healthy Wraps, when I heard the crash of shattering glass.

I looked down the promenade and saw that a huge rectangular piece of glass had fallen from the roof!

People were screaming, running away from the spot where the glass had fallen. I fought the tide, running toward the scene of the accident, to see if anybody needed help. (Both Frank and I have CPR training.)

The glass had fallen right in front of In the Groove, this really cool, funky store. At first the whole area looked clear of people—which was a good thing, believe me. But then I saw that someone was lying on his stomach in the doorway. He was covered in little pieces of glass. Lucky for him it was safety glass, the kind they use in car windshields. When it breaks, it shatters into little round pieces instead of deadly, jagged-edged shards.

As I got closer, I realized, first, that the guy was lying on someone else, and second, that I knew this guy.

"Frank!"

He looked up at me. "Hi, Joe. Am I dead?"

"No, dude—you're still here. Let's just make sure you're okay."

He got up slowly, checking himself for blood, and I saw that the person underneath him was a really cute girl with huge dark eyes. She was clinging to Frank like a barnacle.

Frank helped the girl up, and between sobs, she hugged him, saying, "Thank you!" over and over again, and "You saved my life!"—all of which Frank accepted without an argument.

"You okay, dude?" I asked him.

"I th-think so," he said, still checking himself over.

"You sure seem like you're doing fine," I commented, glancing at the girl.

"Oh. Yeah—Joe, this is Adriana. Adriana, my brother Joe."

"Nice to meet you," she said, nodding at me.

"Likewise."

"I'm, uh, going to be working with her, Joe—here in the store," he explained.

"Ah. Well, good for you."

"What about you—did you get a job?"

"Yeah, but I think you're gonna like yours better," I said, with an eye on Adriana.

Frank was already at work, though—and not the retail kind. He was crouching down at the edge of the pile of glass, looking for clues.

Meanwhile, mall security had arrived, along with the janitor—a weird-looking old guy with OSKAR stitched on his uniform. He was wheeling a large garbage can and carried a big broom over his shoulder.

I looked up at the roof where the huge pane had come loose. The ceiling was high, and the lighting wasn't that good at this hour—but I thought I saw a neat edge of glass around the metal frame of the missing pane. Which made me think that maybe—just maybe—someone had cut through it *on purpose*.

Of course, I couldn't be certain—not from this far away. I needed to get up there on the roof and check it out.

"Everybody back!" shouted the mall security

officer in charge. There weren't very many of us around—mostly store employees, since closing time had come and gone, and the customers with it. In the distance I heard police sirens.

And then I saw Mr. Applegate, running down the promenade toward us from the direction of his office. I could tell right away that he was the most upset person there—even more than Frank and Adriana, who had every right to be scared out of their wits.

Just then, a police whistle blew. "Stand back, everyone!" yelled a voice I recognized instantly as belonging to Chief Ezra Collig—our dad's old friend, and the top man in the Bayport Police Department. The East Side Mall was on the outskirts of town—in his jurisdiction, but just barely.

"Somebody want to tell me what happened?" he asked, looking around at the crowd, most of whom were wearing ID cards identifying them as store employees.

Everyone started answering the chief at once, and he had to blow his whistle again to silence them. "One at a time!" he shouted.

Then he saw me and Frank, and he frowned. "Aw, now, why is it that every time there's trouble, you two are always nearby? No, don't answer that!" he quickly added.

"That skylight came down right on top of us," Frank told the chief, his arm still around the shivering Adriana. "It nearly killed us."

"Hmm," the chief said, scowling. Turning to Officer Con Reilly, another of our pals on the force, he said, "Haven't I been telling you about this place? I get more complaints about conditions here—"

"This was no accident!" Mr. Applegate piped up. "I'm always very careful about safety conditions here—those code violations were all fixed months ago! You can check your records and see."

The chief looked up at the hole in the glass ceiling, then down at the shattered fragments of the skylight, and said, "Looks pretty hazardous to me. But we'll have a look—don't you worry." Turning to Reilly, he added, "Get a detail up on that roof, Con."

"Right, Chief," said Reilly, who took off at a trot, motioning for two other officers to join him.

"If this *was* an accident," the chief said to Applegate, "I'm gonna have to cite you for unsafe conditions. *Again*."

"I'm telling you, sir—this was a message meant for me." Then suddenly Applegate looked up and over my shoulder.

I turned around to see what he was staring at,

and saw a blond-haired woman, soaking wet and about thirty years old. She looked straight out of a sixties movie, with her headband, her vest full of patches and buttons, and her hair in braids. She stared right back at Applegate, with a look on her face somewhere between anger and pleading.

I noticed that one of the buttons on her vest said STEMM. I remembered what Applegate had just said: *This was a message meant for me.*

Then I looked beyond the retro-hippie lady—and there, lurking in the shadows of one of the potted palm trees that lined the promenade, I saw the lawyer for Shangri-La, Bob Meister. He was staring at Applegate too—with a look on his face that said, *I told you so.*

Chief Collig had already started interviewing the witnesses, beginning with Frank and his new "instant girlfriend."

I decided my time would be better spent getting to the roof and seeing what Con Reilly was up to. So I headed for the emergency stairs, which were just to the right of the escalators.

Two flights up, I found the door to the roof. It had been propped open with a cinder block. Its alarm system must have been turned off too, because it hadn't sounded—at least I hadn't heard it, and I have pretty good ears.

Reilly's two men were trying to make their way across the metal frame of the glass roof, keeping their weight off the remaining sheets of glass as they inched their way toward the missing pane.

"Hey, Joe," Reilly greeted me. "Did Chief say it was okay you being up here?"

I had to laugh. "Sure, Con. You know how he loves me poking around his business."

"Ah, that's okay," he said, "seeing as it almost hit Frank, I guess you take a personal interest. Besides, you've saved our bacon more than once. Hey, maybe you'll spot something we don't."

"I doubt that," I said modestly—but it was true. Frank and I have solved more than a few cases for the Bayport Police Department. Chief Collig might not like it, but at least we don't try to take any credit. (ATAC wouldn't let us do that, even if we wanted to. That's how a secret agency stays secret.)

Con's two officers had made it over to the missing panel. "Looks like it was cut through on purpose," one of them called back to us. "Nice clean job—still an edge of glass firmly in place all the way around."

"Geez," Reilly muttered. "If that isn't creepy . . ."

"Hey," I called, moving farther along the framework to a vertical brick wall that had been tarred black. "Check this out, Con."

He came over and stared at it. Then he let out a low whistle. "If that don't beat all," he said.

On the black wall, someone had spray-painted a message, graffiti-style: NEXT TIME DURING BUSINESS HOURS.

It was signed STEMM.

6.
Picking Up the Pieces

The first thing I did after realizing I was still alive was to make sure Adriana was okay. Other than being terrified, she seemed fine, thank goodness. She held on to my arm for a long time, though. I guess it made her feel safer. But the way she was looking at me, it was like I was her hero or something.

Chief Collig finally separated us when he took me aside to question me. I told him everything that had happened—except for the fact that Joe and I had been sent to the mall by ATAC.

He seemed especially interested in Stephanie Flowers, Adriana's boss. I figured he already knew she was involved with STEMM. I was also sure he would run into her hot temper the minute he tried to question her. Chief Collig doesn't like hot tempers, other than his own. So I knew Steph was in trouble.

I thought back to when she'd left us. It couldn't have been more than fifteen minutes from that moment till the glass came crashing down. That would have given her just enough time to get up to the roof and cut through the glass—*if* she had the right cutting tool. But I couldn't see her having enough time to spray the graffiti, too.

I supposed the glass *could* have just fallen by accident, but I didn't think that was likely. When I looked up, it had been coming down in one huge piece, not in broken shards.

While the chief peppered me with questions, I heard police sirens fading into the distance. I knew they were off to find Steph, whom I'd seen briefly in the crowd just after the police had arrived, but not since. Meanwhile, old Mr. Applegate looked like he was having a fit of some kind. He was sitting on the marble edge of the fountain, staring into space, with tears rolling down his wrinkled cheeks.

That poor guy, I thought. *This mall means everything to him.*

The chief was conferring with Detective Wright, who'd been interviewing Oskar, the janitor. "The

60

janitor says there's a bunch of kids that hang out over there by the emergency stairs," Wright was saying. "He says they're always sitting there, right up till closing time. But I looked around—no sign of 'em now, Chief."

"Any names?" the chief asked.

"Not yet, but we're working on it," Wright said. "Should have something for you by tomorrow."

"Okay, we'll concentrate on the STEMM angle for now," the chief decided. "Let's wind this up, eh?"

Chief Collig soon got busy questioning Adriana. I wrote down my cell phone number and passed it to her. "In case you need to reach me," I said, waving good-bye.

I kind of figured she'd call, just to talk it all out. Something like a sheet of glass coming down on you really shakes a person up. It sure had shaken me.

Backing away, I headed for the emergency stairs. I wanted to know more about that group of kids, for one thing. And for another, Joe had gone off this way. I guessed he was up on the roof with Con Reilly, and I was curious what they'd found.

There was a low marble shelf next to the emergency stairs and the escalators. It formed the border for a row of indoor trees. These were bamboo, or some kind of potted palms. They grew pretty high—high enough that a family of sparrows were living up in their crowns. I had no idea how those birds got inside the mall in the first place, but I guessed they ate well—there were plenty of crumbs for them on the floor of the food court.

One of the birds swooped down past me. It landed at the base of a potted tree and started pecking around.

Watching it, I noticed something sticking out of the mulch inside the pot. "Sorry, birdie," I said as it flew away in panic on my approach.

I brushed away the mulch and pulled out a black poncho—the kind that folds up into a pouch you can keep in your pocket. It was wet, and I wondered what it was doing there buried in dry mulch, at the foot of the emergency stairs that led to the roof.

I walked the poncho back over to In the Groove and gave it to Detective Wright, telling him where I'd found it. He thanked me, and I headed back to the stairs.

I stood in front of the marble shelf for a minute, surveying the mall. From here, I could see everything there was to see—the escalators, the second-floor promenade, three ground-floor corridors, the merry-go-round/ball room/kiddie area, and the big fountain that hid the food court.

If I were a kid my age with nothing to do, I'd want to hang out here for sure. Of course, that would never happen. I *always* had something to do.

Like right now.

I started up the stairs, but just then, I heard Joe's distinctive clomping footsteps coming down.

"Frank?"

"Yo," I greeted him. "What'd you find up there?"

"Sabotage—looks pretty professional, too. They must have had a diamond cutting tool. And there's graffiti—a warning from STEMM."

"A warning?"

"'Next time during business hours.'"

I shook my head. "Man, that's some serious stuff. I mean, I've heard of environmentalist groups tying themselves to trees, or lying down under bulldozer treads—but killing innocent people?"

"I agree," said Joe. "Whoever's behind this, there's something extra going on inside their heads— something personal . . . and maybe deadly."

"Well," I said, "that's why we're here. To stop it from happening."

"You got that right. So what'd I miss?"

"They're after a woman named Stephanie Flowers. She owns In the Groove, and she's the president of STEMM. I met her just before it all went down."

"She wouldn't be a blonde, would she? Hippie-looking?" asked Joe.

"That's her. Actually, she's going to be my boss."

"Right, you're going to be working at In the Groove . . . with that girl you introduced me to. Nice going."

"That's Adriana. She kind of helped me get the job."

"Adriana. Nice name." Then Joe froze, remembering something. "Oh, no! I forgot, my job!"

"Oh, yeah, you mentioned that. Where's it at?"

"No, no, I messed up—I was supposed to go back there at closing time!"

"Aw, man, too late now."

He glared at me. "I know that," he said. "I don't need you to tell me I messed up."

"Sorry."

Joe kicked the door open, and we exited the stairwell.

"Hey, I'm sure your boss will understand if you show up tomorrow and explain," I said.

"I don't know," he said. "He's bound to be ticked off."

"Who's 'he,' anyway?"

"The guy from Healthy Wraps."

"You're kidding! You, working at a health-food place?"

"Sure, why not?"

"You *hate* health food."

"I do not. Who says?"

"You *do*. You never want to eat your vegetables."

"I eat them, though—don't I?" Joe insisted.

"Yeah, but—"

"So just lay off me, okay?"

"Whatever, dude."

As we walked back toward In the Groove, I told Joe about the poncho I'd found.

"Sounds like someone wore it up on the roof and then ditched it," he said, looking thoughtful. "Hmm. I guess it didn't work too well."

"Huh?"

"The blonde? She got wet all over anyway."

"Well, I guess with all the wind . . ."

"Yeah, I guess . . ."

We were just passing the food court when Joe pointed toward it.

"I've gotta just go check," he told me. "In case the guy's still there."

"I'll come with you," I said. The thought of watching Joe learning to make a wrap was just too tempting.

But of course, no one was left at the food court. All the stalls had their wire gates pulled down. "Man," Joe said, shaking his head. "I hope I didn't blow it."

"Relax, dude," I told him. "You got one job, you can always get another."

"Easy for you to say. You've *got* a job."

"Maybe—or maybe not. If they arrest Steph, who's to say the shop stays open?"

"You think she really did it?" he asked.

I shrugged. "She was plenty mad about the mall getting sold. And from what you said about the graffiti . . ."

"Yeah, but something about it isn't sitting right," said Joe. He had a look on his face, like he'd swallowed something really bad-tasting. "I can't put my finger on it, but . . ."

"Well *try*," I urged. "What, you think those kids had something to do with it?"

"Maybe. I could see them doing the graffiti, just to get someone else in trouble. But the *glass* . . . The way it was cut, it was too professional for kids like that."

"Well, let's put them on our list for tomorrow."

"List? We've got a list?"

"Sure we do. Let's see. . . . Get here right after school, get me my job back, talk to those kids—if they aren't too scared to show up after all the commotion."

"That's it?"

"No, there's one more thing. One more party we haven't heard from."

"Who's that?"

"The developer who wants to buy the mall," he said. "Shangri-La Enterprises. And their nasty lawyer, too."

"Ah, you've met him?"

"Yup. I think we should make some time to check out what's up over at Shangri-La."

The police were just winding up their investigation when we got back. The photographers were packing up their equipment, and uniformed officers were fencing off the area of the "accident" with yellow crime-scene tape.

"*Now* I can clean up?" Oskar asked Chief Collig.

The chief nodded. "All right, everyone," he called out to the others. "Let's get back to headquarters."

The police packed up and took off, leaving one officer behind to stand guard over the crime scene. Oskar started sweeping up the shards and dumping them into his big garbage can on wheels. Every once in a while, he'd bend down and pick up a big piece, holding it carefully in both hands before dropping it into the can.

He was doing it again now. But wait—that wasn't some big shard of glass he had in his hands. It was something else . . . something shiny, and small enough to fit in his hand.

Oskar examined it closely. He looked up guiltily to see if the cop was watching—which he wasn't. Then Oskar turned and saw me. He quickly stuffed the shiny object into his pocket.

"Hey, Oskar!" I shouted.

Pretending not to hear me, he stuck his broom and dustpan into the can and quickly wheeled it away down the corridor.

"Oskar, wait up!" I yelled, chasing after him. He quickly abandoned the can and broom and kept on running. Far ahead of me, he turned right, into a corridor.

I followed him, but by the time I got there, the corridor was empty, and the doors on either side were locked. I decided I would wait for him to come out, betting that there was no other way he could exit those rooms. I walked back down the corridor to the promenade, stepped out of view, and waited.

Sure enough, a couple of minutes later he tried to sneak out. As he exited the little corridor, I reached out and clapped him on the shoulder.

"Ah!" he cried out, surprised. "What? What you want?"

"You picked something up, over there where the glass came down. I saw you."

"I not take nothing!"

"I *saw* you."

"What, you want search Oskar? Here! Look—see?"

He opened all his pockets, to show me that he wasn't carrying anything—well, except for a dirty hankie and his own wallet. "What, you a policeman or something? What for you follow me? I tell you three times, I not take nothing!"

I had to let him go. He waddled off toward his garbage can and broom. After checking the doors giving off the corridor and finding them both still locked (surprise, surprise), I headed back to where the glass had fallen.

Oskar had sworn up and down that he was innocent. But he'd taken something, all right—something he'd just ditched in one of those little locked rooms. I was sure he would come back and get it later, when no one was watching.

"Whoa," said Joe when I returned. "What was *that* all about?"

"Oskar found something," I said. "Something

he didn't want us, or anybody else, to see."

"Now what could that be?" Joe asked. "I wonder . . ."

"I think we'll have to add Oskar to our little list, Joe."

"I think you're right, Frank. I think, in fact, we'll put him right at the top."

7.
New Angles

"Oh, come on—dish!" Iola was leaning so far over her side of the table she was practically *in* my food tray.

"Easy—down, girl," I said. "I already told you, Chief Collig swore us to secrecy."

"Hey, we're supposed to be your best friends," Chet broke in. He was seated next to Iola, opposite Frank. It was going to be impossible to eat lunch if this inquisition didn't stop soon.

"Yeah, we can keep a secret," said Iola. "What's the matter, don't you trust us?"

"Oh, I trust you, all right," I replied. "I trust you to repeat everything we say, word for word, to every single person you run into between now and doomsday."

"Just answer yes or no," she pleaded, not giving up. "This lady's a member of a terrorist group."

"Define terrorist," I said.

"Oh, come on!" she begged. "Everyone says there are these environmental terrorists looking to blow up the mall!"

"Whoa!" said Frank. "That's a little out there, don't you think?"

"I don't know," Iola said. "What do *you* think?"

"Uh-uh." Frank shook his head, smiling. "Sorry. Nice try, though."

"Rats. Okay," she went on. "Yes or no—the window was broken deliberately."

Frank and I looked at each other. He shrugged. "I guess we can tell them that much," he said.

"Okay. Yes," I revealed.

"Yay! Now we're getting somewhere," said Iola. "Chet? Any questions?"

"Yeah," he said, between bites of his salad. "Do you guys think that bunch of kids who hang out by the stairs at the mall had anything to do with it?"

"We're going to try and check them out this afternoon," Frank told him. "Could very well be."

"'Cause I know someone else it could be," he said.

"Oh yeah? Who?" Frank leaned in closer, paying attention now.

"There's this janitor? I don't know his name, but he's definitely not right in the head. Talks to himself a lot, always looks like he's hiding something . . ."

"He means that guy Oskar," I said to Frank.

"I know that," he said. "Do I look stupid?"

"I think it's those kids with the tattoos," Iola put in. "They give me a hard time every day when I head for the parking lot after my shift."

"Hard time?" I asked. "What do you mean?"

"You know, the usual. Trying to get my attention . . . asking me for my number."

"That's not a crime, Iola," Frank said. "At least, not last time I checked."

"It's not a crime to be so annoying?" she asked. "Well, if it isn't, it should be."

"At least they're not as weird as that janitor," Chet insisted. "I don't understand why the police didn't take him in for questioning. I mean, who has the keys to the roof? *He* does."

"Apparently, whoever did it used Mr. Applegate's keys," Frank told them. "He reported them missing from his office drawer last night."

"So let's see," Iola summed up. "We've got the

janitor, those kids, and that lady environmentalist. Any other suspects?"

"Actually, there is one other guy I've yet to check out," I commented.

"Oh, yeah?" Iola said. "Okay, give." She batted her eyelashes at me, smiling.

"He's this lawyer for a big development corporation. I heard him sort of threatening Mr. Applegate if he didn't sell the mall."

"Sort of? Hmm," Iola said. "What do you mean by that?"

"You know how lawyers are," I said. "They can threaten without threatening."

She rolled her eyes. "I don't know, but I can't picture a lawyer in a fancy suit climbing up onto the roof to cut that glass."

"Why not?" asked Chet. "Just because lawyers wear suits doesn't mean they're afraid of getting dirty."

"Or playing dirty tricks," I added. "We're going over to see him right after school."

After school Frank and I walked out to the parking lot and got on our bikes. As he was about to strap on his helmet, he said, "You know, I think maybe I ought to go straight over to the mall and see what's going on down there."

So we split up, and I pointed my wheels toward downtown Bayport—specifically the Shangri-La Building, a gleaming glass skyscraper on the corner of Main and Broad.

First I checked the directory on the wall. I saw that Bob Meister's office was on the thirty-fourth floor. I also saw that the president of Shangri-La Enterprises, LLC, was a Mr. Ralph Eberhardt, whose office was on thirty-five.

There was a security guard in the lobby, manning a velvet rope that barred the way in for anyone who didn't have a magnetic ID card. I went up to him and said, "Hi, I'm here to see Mr. Bob Meister."

"Is he expecting you?"

"Um, I'm not sure. I mean, yes, he's expecting me, but not right at this moment. Could you see if he's free?"

The guard punched in a number on his phone. "Name?"

"Hardy. Joe Hardy. I'm here on behalf of Mr. Arthur Applegate. It's about the East Side Mall."

The guard put the phone down. "Sorry, he's not picking up," he reported.

"Oh, that's all right," I said. "I'll just go up and leave a note with his secretary."

He frowned, considering this. "I guess that'd

be all right," he said, handing me a stick-on pass. "Thirty-fourth floor."

"Thanks so much." I slapped the pass onto my shirt and hurried to the elevator before he changed his mind.

I was going to push thirty-four, but then I thought better of it. Meister wasn't picking up, so he probably wasn't there anyway. Besides, I wanted to see his boss even more. I pushed thirty-five instead—the top floor.

The bell chimed, the doors slid open, and I walked over to a huge, gleaming reception desk. Behind it sat an older woman with granny glasses and frosted hair that was somewhere between gray and blue.

"Hello," I said, going up to her. "I'm here to see Mr. Eberhardt."

"Do you have an appointment?" the receptionist asked, looking me up and down. I'm sure I didn't look to her like someone who'd have an appointment with her boss.

"Not exactly," I replied. "I'm here about the East Side Mall deal. I'm, um, connected with Mr. Applegate, the mall's current owner, and I just need a few minutes of Mr. Eberhardt's time."

"He's a very busy man."

"Oh, of course. I do appreciate that," I said.

"Perhaps if you left your card, he could get back to you?"

"Oh, I'm afraid that won't work," I told her. "It's very, er, time-sensitive. I just need to see him for a minute, actually. Is he . . . in there?" I asked, indicating the corner office.

She'd been around way too long to fall for that one, but I could tell that my hunch was right, because she stood right up and positioned herself between me and the big oak door that led to the corner office.

"He's in a meeting right now," she said. "But let me find out if he's able to see you afterward." She put one hand on the doorknob. "Wait right here," she added, and disappeared inside.

Well, I knew full well that he wasn't going to agree to see me. After all, who was I to him, anyway? Oh, sure, I'd dropped Applegate's name— but this Eberhardt guy was a real big man, and he wouldn't be talking to anyone except Applegate himself, I was sure.

So I did the only thing I could do in the situation. Instead of waiting for the receptionist to come out, I followed her in.

When I slipped through the doorway, she was leaning over her boss's desk with her back to me, whispering something—no doubt about my being there.

I couldn't see who she was talking to, but I didn't need to. Eberhardt's office spoke for him—loudly. It was humongous, with glass walls looking out over Bayport and the bay itself. I could even see the East Side Mall in the distance, over beyond the marsh.

I cleared my throat to let them know I was there. The receptionist spun around so fast I thought she was going to drill a hole in the floor. She gasped in surprise and horror. "Sir, I asked you to wait in the reception area!"

"It's all right, Madge. I'll handle this."

Behind the receptionist rose Mr. Ralph Eberhardt, president of Shangri-La Enterprises, LLC. He was tall and well polished—everything from his perfectly groomed silver hair, to his thousand-dollar suit, to the ultrawhite smile pasted on his face. "What can I do for you, Mr. . . ."

"Hardy. Joe Hardy." I strode right up to his desk, offering my hand.

Madge stepped aside, frowning, then marched out of the room, leaving the door open behind her.

Eberhardt gripped my hand and squeezed it so hard I couldn't believe it. The pain was intense as my knuckles were ground into each other with the relentless force of his iron grip.

"Now, Mr. Hardy—what can I do for you?"

"You can let go of my hand, for starters."

Lucky for me, he did. "It's rude, you know, to barge into someone's office like this."

"I'm sorry, sir—but I knew you wouldn't see me otherwise."

"And how did you come to that conclusion?"

I didn't answer that one—it was way too tricky. He had me cornered! What was I going to say to make him talk to me?

One more glance around the room gave me my answer. There, on the wall above Eberhardt's desk, was a plaque from the Bayport Policemen's Benevolent Association, thanking him for his generous contributions.

"My dad is Fenton Hardy. Maybe you've heard of him?"

In Bayport, this is a trick that sometimes works to get me and Frank into places we could never enter otherwise. It worked this time too. I hate to pull rank, but our father knows a lot of Bayport bigwigs.

"*Fenton Hardy*? My gosh, I was in his foursome last month, at the charity golf tournament for the Policemen's Benevolent Association!"

Eberhardt's face relaxed into a more human smile, and he clapped me hard on the shoulder. "Wonderful fellow. Chief Collig says he was the best man the New York City Police Department ever had!"

He sat back down. "Come to think of it, you *look* a lot like him. Well, Joe—any son of Fenton Hardy's is welcome here."

"Thanks," I said, still rubbing my sore hand.

"Sit down, sit down," he said, indicating a chair. "So what brings you here, Joe?" All of a sudden, he was as friendly as could be.

I sat down, but I didn't smile back. My hand still hurt—and the scary first impression he'd made was still impressing me.

"I believe Fenton actually mentioned you . . . and your brother, too. If I remember correctly, he said you were quite the amateur detectives."

"Yes . . . well . . . I'm actually here about something else."

"Oh, good," he said, chuckling. "I thought maybe you were here to investigate a crime!"

I laughed along with him, but not too hard. "I have this job after school at the East Side Mall— and I heard rumors that Shangri-La was planning to buy it."

He stiffened, and the phony smile was suddenly pasted back onto his face. "And?"

"Well, is it true?" I asked.

"May I ask, just where did you hear that?"

"I, um . . ." Aw, man—he'd gone and turned it around on me! Suddenly *I* was the one on the spot. "I dunno. Some kids were talking about it, and how the marsh was going to get paved over and stuff."

He laughed, without opening his mouth. "That mosquito-infested disease incubator? I'll tell you what, Joe—whoever paves that filthy marsh over should be awarded the key to the city. It's a first-class health hazard."

"Um, well, some people say there are endangered species there."

"Ever hear of dengue fever? Malaria? West Nile virus? Encephalitis? All diseases bred by mosquitoes."

"They could spray for them, I guess," I suggested.

"What, and kill the endangered tadpoles?" He laughed again and held out his palms to me. "You see, Joe—there are two sides to every story."

"At *least* two," I agreed.

"Now, if—and I stress the word *if*—Shangri-La were to make an offer on a property like the East Side Mall, it would only be with the idea of transforming a run-down section of Bayport into a new, world-class shopping showplace—a destination for all the better elements of society."

"Oh, that's another thing I heard," I said. "I heard that if your company builds a new mega-mall there, teens aren't going to be allowed after dark."

He slammed his huge hand down on the table, so hard that I flinched in my chair. "Now, you see? Someone goes and starts spreading rumors, and all of a sudden, the air is filled with vicious lies!"

"So you wouldn't be keeping teens out?"

"Of *course* not!" he said, forcing the smile back onto his lips. "Teens would be welcome, even after dark—so long as they're accompanied by an adult."

Aha! So it *was* true!

"And since you've heard so much, I assume you've also heard that some group of wacky enviro-nuts is threatening violence to stop any deal."

"I . . . yes, I did hear something like that."

He nodded. "These people will do anything, Joe, to protect their precious turtles, snails, tadpoles—whatever. As long as it's not *people*! Here at Shangri-La, we care about people first and foremost." He sat back in his chair and looked me over to see if I was buying his argument.

I didn't know what to think, to tell you the truth.

I heard what he was saying, and it made sense, kind of. Still, I knew that it wasn't only mosquitoes living in that marsh. And when he said that about teens having to be accompanied by an adult—well, if you're a teen, you know how most of us would feel about having to be chaperoned every time we wanted to go to the mall.

He opened a drawer of his desk and took out a photograph, handing it to me. "There," he said. "See that bug? That's what they're trying so hard to save! Can you believe it?"

It was a pretty ugly bug, I had to admit. Lots of eyes and legs and feelers. Still, if it was a dying breed . . .

"Hey, I have an idea," I suggested. "If Shangri-La buys the mall and builds their project, how about adding a teen center to it, so kids my age have someplace fun and safe to hang out and shop?"

"*Shop*? Kids don't *shop*! They just 'hang out,' as you call it—not buying anything, and scaring away people who have real money to spend!"

"Now wait a second, Mr. Eberhardt," I said. "I know lots of kids who have their parents' credit cards and buy tons of stuff."

He laughed that closed-mouth laugh again. "Not the kind of expensive merchandise *I* mean to sell."

"So you *are* planning to buy the mall and make it over!"

"I'm not saying that. It's just a 'what-if' at this point."

By this time, I was kind of ticked off at him. "But really, Mr. Eberhardt, your plan isn't about doing something good for people—it's all about money, isn't it?"

His smile vanished, and he looked me right in the eyes. "Isn't *everything*, Joe?"

Eberhardt punched a button on his phone. I figured he was buzzing his receptionist, but I didn't hear a sound coming from the reception area outside the office.

I turned toward the doorway, expecting to see the receptionist come in to escort me out. Instead, Bob Meister appeared. When he saw me, his face grew dark with suspicion.

"Bob, is this the young fellow you told me about yesterday?" Eberhardt asked him.

"It sure is," Meister answered.

"You know, Joe, I have a lot of respect for your father. But that doesn't mean I'm going to put up with his son snooping around my business, especially when it's got nothing to do with him. I understand that, being the son of a famous lawman, you're naturally curious about all sorts of

SUSPECT PROFILE

Name: Ralph Eberhardt

Hometown: Boston, MA

Physical description: Age 50, 6'4", 220 lbs. Well-groomed, well-dressed, in good shape for his age. Tall, manicured, and very impressive.

Occupation: President and chief executive officer of Shangri-La Enterprises, LLC.

Background: From one of the old families, he grew up in Boston, went to the best private schools, attended Harvard and Wharton Business School, then rose to the top of the business world. Moved to Bayport to start his own real estate development company, Shangri-La. Now owns lots of buildings and properties in and around town, as well as other places, and is hungry for more. He is also a big contributor to Bayport charities, including the PBA, vets, firefighters, and EMS. Last year he was given the key to the city for the new playground he donated to Bayport.

Suspicious behavior: His tactics to buy the East Side Mall sure look shady—especially the fact that he has a guy like Meister doing his dirty work.

Suspected of: Setting up a situation where Applegate will have to sell the mall to him.

Possible motives: Money, money, and more money. Oh, yeah—and power, too.

things. But a word of friendly advice—it would be smart for you to stay out of this."

I stood up. "Are you threatening me, Mr. Eberhardt?"

He walked around his desk and stood in front of me, our faces only inches apart. "Threatening you? Good heavens, no! Just giving you a friendly word of advice, Joe. There are dangerous people out there who would do anything to stop the sale of the East Side Mall. And I do mean *anything*."

He stuck his hand out, but I didn't take it—he'd already squeezed my fingers into powder once, and once was enough.

"Have a nice day, Joe," he said. "And give my best regards to your father. Bob will escort you out."

Meister gestured toward the door, and I went out, with him right behind me. I kept going, past the reception area to the elevator bank, where I pressed the down button and waited.

"You'd better keep away from here," Meister warned, just loudly enough for me to hear. "And from the mall, too, if you know what's good for you. Is that clear?"

The elevator door opened. I stepped inside, then turned to face him. As the doors closed, I smiled and said, "Clear as glass, Mr. Meister."

8.

Up on the Roof

It looked like rain, so I parked my bike in the indoor parking deck, then headed inside to the mall. The human traffic was pretty heavy for that time of day. I figured lots of people were curious after reading the papers that morning.

In fact, there was quite a crowd gathered outside In the Groove. Above them a large blue tarp hid the roof where the glass had fallen. There was a drain in the tarp, hooked up to a long hose that ended in a huge trash can—Oskar's improvised flood control, I guessed.

The whole area under the tarp was roped off, and a mall security guard was trying to keep people away from the store's entrance. "Move along, please, everyone," he kept saying—but nobody listened.

There was Adriana, craning her neck as though she were looking for someone. "Hey!" I called out, waving.

She brightened when she saw me, but she still looked scared and anxious. "Hey, Frank," she said, giving me a kiss on the cheek as I reached her. "Have you seen Steph?"

"Uh, no," I answered, disappointed as I realized it wasn't me she'd been looking for.

"I'm worried," she said. "She's never late. And after last night . . ."

"Let me see if I can track her down." I took out my cell phone and pushed number five on speed dial.

It picked up after one ring. "Police headquarters. Officer Reilly here."

"Con? It's Frank Hardy."

"Oh, hello, Frank. How're you feelin'? Still a little stunned, I'll bet."

"No, I'm okay," I assured him. "I'm trying to find out what happened to that woman you were looking for. Stephanie Flowers? You know, the one with STEMM?"

"Oh, her—she's a piece of work, I'll tell you. Yeah, we caught up with her pretty quick. She was at her apartment, but she tried to knock out the two rookies I sent to bring her in. Nearly caught one of 'em on the chin, too—they had to cuff her, hands and feet."

"Wow. She must have been pretty upset," I said.

"Well, I guess!" exclaimed Reilly. "Anyways, we booked her on conspiracy charges."

"*What?*"

"And she's mighty lucky we didn't throw in resisting arrest," he added.

"What was the evidence for conspiracy?" I asked.

"Well, to begin with, she's not just a *part* of this enviro-nut group, she's apparently the head of it, or at least one of the leaders. So that makes her responsible, at least for the graffiti."

"Aw, come on, Con—that's just circumstantial."

"Agreed, Frank, but it's still pretty clear-cut—especially when you factor in that poncho."

"Oh, yeah? What about it?"

"We found a couple of long blond hairs inside the hood, residue of glass powder on the sleeves, and a diamond-tipped cutting tool in the pocket. Oh, yeah, and the poncho was a women's medium. How's that for evidence?"

"Whoa." I had to admit, it looked pretty bad for my new boss. I felt awful about it—not just because she seemed like a nice lady who really cared about the environment, but because Adriana might lose her job now.

"Is she still there?" I asked Reilly.

"Why, you want to interrogate her?" He laughed, knowing that police work was in my blood.

"Actually, she's my new boss here at the mall."

"No kidding! Since when?"

"Since yesterday. About fifteen minutes before the glass came down."

"Hmm. What a coincidence. . . . It couldn't be that you and your brother were nosing around this case, could it?"

"Hey," I said, "it costs money to keep bikes like ours. We need jobs."

"I've seen them bikes," he told me, "and you've got a point there. You and Joe be careful on 'em, you hear?"

"We will. Thanks, Con."

"Anyway, the Flowers dame isn't here. Somebody posted bail for her—she's free till the grand jury convenes."

"Really? Who bailed her out, do you know?"

"Ah, I was down at the doughnut shop when it happened. Let me check—can you hold on a second?"

"Sure thing. Take your time."

While I waited, I filled Adriana in.

"But that's so wrong!" she said in a loud whisper, trying to keep our conversation private even though there were dozens of people milling around. "There's no way Steph would do something like that—I *know* her!"

Unfortunately, you hear that a lot in detective work. All those people who think they "know" the accused are usually dead wrong.

"Frank?"

"Yes, Con?"

"A messenger came in with the bond, posted in the name of AA Associates."

"AA Associates? That's not very helpful, is it?"

"Sorry. Maybe you can track them down, though. You and Joe are pretty good at that sort of thing, last I heard."

"Okay—thanks for your help."

"Yeah, sure thing. And sorry about your job, but you'll find another. Hey, come to think of it, they're hiring down at the doughnut shop!"

"Uh, thanks, but no thanks," I said, and ended the call. "Okay," I told Adriana. "Now what?"

"Frank?"

"Yeah?"

"I was just thinking . . . if Steph's not with the police, and she's not here . . . then where *is* she?"

I shrugged. "At home, maybe?"

"She would have called and told me not to come

91

in," Adriana said. "She would have called you, too, if she had your number."

"Okay, well, maybe she's meeting with her group—you know, an emergency STEMM strategy session to figure out her defense, get legal help, that kind of thing?"

"I guess . . ."

"That's *if* she's innocent. If she isn't . . ."

"Frank!"

"Just supposing . . . she might have skipped bail and left town for good."

"No possible way. Like I said, I know her. Steph cares way too much about this place to run away."

"I wonder who AA Associates are," I said. "I think I'll do a little Internet search tonight." Something the police should have been doing, of course. But they were sure they had this case solved—why should they even care who posted Steph's bail?

As for me, my mind was still open. There were too many angles to this case, and too many suspicious characters around it, for me to close the books so fast.

Still, I had to admit that it looked bad for Steph. When it comes to crimes, ninety-nine out of a hundred times the obvious answer is the right one.

And so far, all the actual evidence was pointing to one person—my new and possibly former boss.

"Have you got a key to the store?" I asked Adriana.

"Uh-huh. Why?"

"Let's go in."

"Now?"

"Right now."

"Move along, please," the security guy told us as we ducked under the ropes and made for the door of the store.

"She works here," I explained, pointing to Adriana. "And we need to go inside to get the purse she left here yesterday—in all the commotion, she forgot to take it with her."

"Yeah, I understand," he said, "but I can't let anybody in there."

"Come on, pal." I clapped him on the shoulder. "Look, she's got a key, okay? She wouldn't have a key if she didn't work here."

He made a face. "I guess it'd be okay," he said reluctantly. "But no hanging around in there. If Mr. Applegate comes around, I could get in trouble."

"We'll be right out. Promise," I said, and we ducked inside the store before he could change his mind.

When we were inside, I turned to Adriana. "Did

Steph own a rain poncho?" I asked her.

"A poncho?"

"Yeah, you know, the kind that folds up into a little bag?"

"I . . . think so," she said, trying to remember. "You know, she did have this black one she used to hang in the storeroom. I remember she'd put it on when deliveries came in through the back and it was raining."

Then it hit me. "It was raining yesterday. Remember? She came out, said she was leaving, then she looked up at the skylight—at the piece of glass that came down fifteen minutes later—and she said, 'It's starting to pour.' "

"It was, too," Adriana said, nodding.

"So why wasn't she wearing the poncho?"

"I don't know . . . maybe she hadn't taken it out of her purse yet."

"But you said it used to hang on the hook in the storeroom."

She gasped. "That's right!" she said.

We ran back to the storeroom. "That's the door that leads to the loading dock," Adriana said, pointing to it. "And that's the hook she used to hang the poncho on."

"Now, I found it over by the stairs leading to the roof. But if Steph saw it was pouring and didn't have it in her bag, why didn't she come back in here to get it?"

"I have no idea," Adriana said.

"Maybe . . . just maybe, it was because *she knew it wasn't here!*"

"But if she didn't have it on her, it *would* have been here, Frank."

"Not if someone else had taken it earlier."

"But who would do that?"

"I don't know," I admitted. "I'm just saying it's possible."

"Frank?"

"Yeah?"

"Will you take me up there?"

"To the roof?"

"Uh-huh."

"Wh-what for?"

"I want to see it."

"Why?"

"Because until I do, there's no way I'll believe Steph did this."

The truth was, I wanted to go up there myself. When you're trying to picture how a crime was committed, and what sort of person could have done it, there's no better place than the crime scene itself. And so far, only Joe had seen it.

We left the store, thanked the security guard,

and walked down the promenade. There was that same bunch of kids, sitting on the low marble shelf by the emergency stairs.

I counted seven of them: Five guys, two girls.

They were staring at us, and I didn't like the look in their eyes. I couldn't help feeling they were sizing us up. Targeting us, almost.

My guess was that the police had already taken these kids in and questioned them—pretty harshly, no doubt. That could explain why they looked so ticked off.

Still, there was something about them that creeped me out as we opened the stairway door and left them behind. I could feel their eyes on us right up till the moment the metal door slammed shut.

I held Adriana's hand and guided her up the two flights of stairs to the roof. We got there, only to find the emergency door shut.

"Don't worry," I said, fishing out my lock-picking contraption.

"Won't the alarm go off?"

"I've got that covered," I said, placing a magnetic disk on the alarm box. The disk was a gift from ATAC, given to me and Joe for use on a previous case (some things are just too good to return when the case is closed).

The disk sent out interference to jam the alarm's frequency and disable it while I picked the lock.

"We're good to go," I stated, pushing the door open.

Out on the roof, nothing had changed. The hole in the skylight was still there—which made me think that maybe this mall *deserved* to get sold to the highest bidder. After all, any self-respecting shopping center would have had it replaced by now, instead of just putting up a tarp.

The graffiti was still there too. Silver paint, I noted. Then I noticed something else. . . .

"Hey," I said to Adriana. "See where it says STEMM?"

"Yeah?"

"Look—the Ms don't interlock!"

Her eyes widened. "If it were written by a STEMM member, they would have known how to draw their own logo."

Just then the stairway door banged open behind us. The buzz-cut brigade emerged onto the roof one by one, until all seven of them were blocking our only exit.

"Yo," called the tallest of the boys. "What are you doing up here?"

"I could ask you the same question," I said.

"Go ahead. Ask."

"Okay. What are you doing up here?"

"Following you," he replied.

"I'm Frank Hardy. This is my friend, Adriana. And you are . . . ?"

He seemed caught off balance. I think he expected me to come flying at him with both fists—I think he would have *liked* that. But now he had to *think*—something he obviously wasn't used to.

"Paul," he said, giving me a little nod. "Paul Burns."

None of the others answered. "Well, now that we've been introduced," I said, "what did you have in mind?"

"Huh?" Burns was obviously the leader, because no one else even tried to answer.

"I mean, are you looking for a fight? Or did you just come up here to chat?"

I was already rolling up my sleeves, getting ready to put my martial arts skills to good use, and hoping none of these kids had been to the gym recently.

"That depends," he said warily.

"On what?" I asked.

"On what *you're* doing up here."

"Oh. Okay. We're checking out the scene of the crime."

"Crime?" he said, tensing. "I heard it was just an accident."

"No way," I told him. "No. Somebody cut that glass."

His eyes shifted nervously. Then he pointed at the graffiti. "It says right there who did it."

"I'm not so sure," I said.

"Then who did?"

"*You* tell *me*," I said. "Maybe it was you."

Now they were *all* looking really, really tense.

"They did it, Frank," said Adriana, positioning herself behind an air vent for protection. "Look at their guilty faces. Can't you see it?"

I saw it, all right.

"Says who?" Burns snarled, stepping right up to me and pointing his finger in my face.

I grabbed the finger, hard, and twisted it around.

"Yeow!" he shouted, and his friends all surged forward, ready for a fight.

I held up Paul's finger, the tip showing, and they all suddenly froze in place.

"Couldn't get the silver paint off your trigger finger, could you, Paul?" I asked. "The color matches perfectly—notice?"

He yanked his hand free and whipped it behind his back. "You can't prove a thing!" he said.

SUSPECT PROFILE

Name: Paul Burns

Hometown: East side of Bayport

Physical description: Age 17, 6' 1", 190 lbs. Tattoos, piercings, buzz cut, ripped cargo pants, dirty T-shirt, mean look in his beady eyes.

Occupation: Hanging out and making trouble.

Background: From a broken, abusive home. Has been thrown out of school three times already, and the third time stuck. He now contemplates his future while hanging out at the mall.

Suspicious behavior: That silver finger says it all, doesn't it?

Suspected of: Spraying graffiti implicating STEMM, cutting glass on roof.

Possible motives: Getting even with the world, maybe?

"I already have—and I have a witness. Right, Adriana?"

"Right."

They all started looking at one another, desperate

for a way out. Finally Paul said, "Look, everybody's into something, you know? Some people lift stuff from stores. Some people key cars. At least graffiti doesn't hurt anyone!"

"And what have you got against STEMM?" asked Adriana. "What did they ever do to you?"

"Nothin'," Paul said. "I just added that part on my own."

"Wait—what do you mean?" I asked. "The rest wasn't your idea?"

"No, man. We got paid."

"You got paid?"

"Hey, everything costs money. If somebody offers you a job for money, you take it, right?"

"Uh, not really," I told him. "Not if it's illegal."

He laughed. "I'll get off. I'm a minor, and I was talked into it."

"By who?" I asked. "Who paid you to do this?"

"Oh, no," he said, smiling and wagging a finger at me as his buddies sniggered. "None of your business."

"Okay," I said. "Maybe the police can convince you to tell them."

He shook his head slowly. "Not a chance," he said, his eyes boring into mine. "Some things are worse than going to jail, man. *Much* worse."

"Paul, they've already arrested somebody else

for cutting that glass, and that person may go to prison for it. If you did it, and they find out you tried to make someone else look guilty, you'll definitely go away—for a long, long time."

"We didn't do the glass!" he yelled. "Just the graffiti, man—not the glass."

I blew out a big breath. "Okay," I said. "Then if it wasn't you, who was it?"

Paul looked at his friends, and they looked back at him. "How should I know, man? Like I told you, we just got paid to do the graffiti, that's all."

"And when was that?"

"I don't know, around six, I guess. We got done just before it started raining. You can't paint on a wet surface, you know? It drips."

He was right. The graffiti had to have been sprayed earlier. That would have given Steph enough time to come up here and cut the glass, for sure.

But had she done it?

"I'll ask you one more time, Paul," I said. "Who paid you?"

He stared me down, but I could tell he was a little shaky. His eyes were darting left and right, trying to find a way out of the mess he knew he was in.

"Okay," he finally said. "I'll tell you. It was

that lady from In the Groove. She paid us—but I messed her up good."

He laughed again, pointing to the word STEMM. It was a mean laugh, but tinged with relief. "Yeah, it was her—the blonde with the funky jacket. You know, with all the buttons." He nodded, staring at his handiwork sprayed on the wall. "I'll bet she cut the glass, too."

His friends were looking at him in shock, and so was Adriana. "He's lying, Frank! Can't you see he's lying?"

I shook my head. Paul Burns might have been lying, or he might have been telling the truth. But either way, things sure looked bad for Steph.

9.
Murder at the Mall

"What do you mean, I should still hire you? Where were you yesterday?"

I felt like tearing my hair out. I mean, my assignment from ATAC was to get a job—*any stupid job*—at the East Side Mall. Not too complicated. But so far, I seemed to be a complete bust. I couldn't even *give* myself away!

I'd been here at the food court for ten minutes already, trying every excuse I could come up with to convince Clem Bartlett to give me another chance. Too bad for me, he turned out to be a stickler for being on time.

"But I was on my way here when I heard the glass shattering."

"Oh, yeah? That was ten minutes past closing

104

time. You were already ten minutes late! I've got a business to run here. I can't put up with workers who don't know what time it is."

"But—"

"What time is it?"

"Huh?"

"What time is it?"

"It's, um . . ."

"It's time for me to get back to work. You should try it sometime."

"I *am* trying!" I shouted.

Everyone turned around. I could see Chet and Iola leaning forward in their food stalls. Everyone and his brother wanted to get a peek at the argument and see whether it would turn into a full-blown fistfight.

"Hey, I'm offering a *week of free labor*, remember? And I know how to sell wraps! You give me a chance, and I'll turn this lousy business around for you."

I could tell he was ticked at me, but at least I'd gotten his attention. "Okay, smart guy. I'll give you ten minutes, starting right now. Let's see what you can do."

"Deal!"

I leaped right over the counter and grabbed the uniform he handed me. In no time, I was decked out in green apron, orange shirt, and white paper hat, ready to go.

The only problem was, I'd been giving him a load of baloney. I had no earthly idea how to sell a Healthy Wrap.

"Hey, get your wraps here!" I called out to the passing shoppers. "Healthy Wraps!"

No one stopped. Once they realized there wasn't going to be a fight, Healthy Wraps didn't interest them. If I wanted to keep this job, I had exactly five minutes to come up with something really, really good.

And then it came to me. Suddenly I knew what to do. I grabbed one of the wraps that was sitting under the glass as a display item and took a huge bite out of it.

"Mmmm!" I said, nodding happily as I chewed and chewed. "Mmm-mm-mmm!"

A few of the passing shoppers stopped to watch. None of them had ever seen a food court employee stuffing his face with his own food before.

"Is it that good?" asked a lady lugging two big shopping bags.

I nodded enthusiastically, swallowing. Then I tore off another huge bite of what I can only describe as day-old plastic, flavored with wax.

No, it wasn't because Clem's wraps tasted

106

bad. It was because the wraps he'd laid out for display had been laminated by soaking them in plastic!

Why didn't he warn me? I thought, too late. Clem was practically rolling on the floor, laughing his head off and pointing at me.

As I swallowed my second mouthful of laminated food, I promised myself that once this case was over with, I'd come back and make Clem eat one of these too.

Sometimes, though, you just have to grin and bear it. I bit off yet another mouthful and asked the lady if she wanted one.

"Sure, why not?" she said. "I'm not much into health food myself. But if the guy behind the counter is eating it, it must be good!"

I handed her a wrap—a real one, courtesy of Clem—and watched as she bit right into it. "Yummy!" she squealed. "Hey, Irma, you've gotta try one of these!"

Her friend scurried over, followed by a couple of curious onlookers—and by the time my ten minutes was up, half the food court was lined up to try Clem Bartlett's Healthy Wraps.

"Eating one *myself*! I've gotta admit, kid, I never thought of that!" He clapped me on the back, laughing some more.

"I assume this means I'm hired," I said, thinking thoughts of murder.

"Oh, you're hired, all right," he said. "Keep up the great work. Ha ha ha!"

I would have hauled off and socked him right there, but—well, what can I say? I needed the job. Besides, I wasn't feeling so good.

I worked the stand until closing time. As the mall emptied out, I sat at one of the food court tables with Iola and Chet, waiting for Frank to show up and my stomach to calm down.

"Plastic—that's funny!" said Chet, doubling over.

"Go ahead, laugh," I said with a groan. "I'd be laughing myself if I wasn't so nauseous."

Frank came walking down the promenade from the direction of the parking deck.

"Where were you?" I asked him.

"I wanted to walk Adriana to her car," he explained. "She's still freaked out by what happened yesterday."

"You guys, I've gotta book," Iola told us. "I have a chemistry test tomorrow."

"Yeah, me too," Chet said, getting up with her. "Come on, I'll walk you to your car. You guys coming?"

"Uh, not yet," answered Frank. "I've got to show Joe something here first."

"Okay, see you tomorrow, then," Chet said.

"Bye," called Iola, leaving with him.

"Joe," Frank said in a low voice when they were gone, "I've got some big news."

"Fire away," I said.

He told me about the poncho belonging to Stephanie Flowers, and about the kids with the tattoos and piercings spraying the graffiti.

"And you know this *how?*"

"They spray-painted the STEMM logo all wrong. Adriana noticed it too."

"Dude," I said, "you'd better leave her out of this. It's getting too dangerous for spectators."

"She's already in it, Joe. She nearly got killed yesterday, remember?"

"I guess you're right," I replied. "But how'd you get them to confess?"

"I saw the silver paint on the kid's trigger finger."

"Brilliant," I said. "What else did you find out?"

"Well, they said Steph paid them to do it, but they double-crossed her by signing it STEMM. They said they did the spraying before closing time, and they denied knowing who cut the glass."

"Seems pretty obvious, doesn't it?"

109

"I don't know," he said slowly. "Wouldn't she have noticed that the graffiti wasn't what she'd paid for?"

"It was raining hard when the glass was cut," I pointed out. "And she was probably wearing that poncho, with the hood up. She might have missed spotting the word STEMM."

"Or maybe it was somebody else," Frank suggested. "Somebody who wanted Steph to take the fall."

"That would mean those kids are lying about who paid them," I said.

"Stranger things have been known to happen," he argued. "You know, at first, when I grabbed the kid's finger, he said he wouldn't tell me who paid them. He said some things were worse than going to jail. But then, after that, he changed his mind and decided to tell me after all."

"So?"

"Joe, maybe he *didn't* add the word STEMM on his own—maybe he was paid by somebody else to put it there."

"It's possible," I had to admit. "Hmm. Maybe if the police grill those kids . . ."

"They'll just deny it," he said. "I mean, the part about being paid. They're juveniles, so they won't go to jail just for spraying graffiti."

"There must be another way we can get them to cooperate," I said. "Meanwhile, I've got an idea who else might have paid them."

I told him about my visit to Shangri-La, and my run-in with Bob Meister.

"Joe, this thing is not over by a long shot," Frank stated. "Whoever cut that glass is getting ready for round two. And we've got to prevent it."

"It?"

"Whatever they're about to pull. Steph is out on bail, and no one knows where she is. So if she's the criminal, she's on the loose. And if she's not, and someone's trying to make her look guilty, they'll try to strike while she has no alibi."

"You mean, like right now?"

"Tonight would be about ideal, wouldn't you say?"

I had to agree with him. "So what do we do?"

"We camp out here at the mall," he said. "In hiding, of course. We see what happens, and if anything goes down, we get in the way of it."

"Sounds like a plan."

"I just wish I'd gotten something to eat before closing time," said Frank.

"Not me." I shook my head. "I couldn't eat a thing if you paid me."

We took up positions, straggling along with the

last of the shoppers as they left for the parking garage. Frank positioned himself by the stairs to the roof, in case that gang of kids made an appearance or someone tried to get up there again.

It was a good position. There were trees and concrete pillars to hide behind, and he had a good view in three directions out of four.

As for me, I headed to the area near Mr. Applegate's office. I'd had luck in that area before, and I figured, why not try it again? It was one of the few parts of the mall Frank couldn't keep an eye on.

I found a spot to settle in—a little vestibule fronting a maintenance closet—and waited. It wasn't five minutes before I heard a door closing nearby. Keys jangled, and then I heard footsteps.

"Never mind that, where are you? And what have you done?"

It was Applegate, talking to someone on his cell phone!

"Of course I'm angry! I know we haven't been on good terms lately. But as long as I'm alive, this is still my property, not yours! I can do whatever I want with it. Do you think you can get your way by threats and violence? Well, if you're trying to scare me out of it, you must have lost your senses!"

He listened for a minute, then said, "How am I supposed to believe that? You know, I wanted to keep this private, but your outrageous behavior is making it impossible!"

He listened again, and I could see his shoulders slump and soften. "Oh, very well," he grumbled. "I'll hold off for another twenty-four hours. But unless you can prove it, I'll have no other choice. I have my own future to think of—and yours, too."

He flipped his phone shut, took out a hankie, and blew his nose. I got the impression he was actually *crying*. Then he opened his phone again and punched in another number.

"It's me," he muttered. "Yes, me. I called to say I need more time . . . twenty-four hours . . . to clear up some family business."

He closed up his phone, stuffed it into his pocket, and hurried off down the promenade.

Interesting. He'd been talking to two different people, obviously. But who?

I was curious to know more, so I followed Mr. Applegate at a safe distance. He crossed the empty food court area, then turned right at the fountain and headed for the parking deck.

As I followed him, I saw that the food court wasn't quite empty after all—Oskar was standing with his broom, eating a Phrank and chatting with Phil. He seemed to be in a great mood for once.

"I going be rich, lots money!" he said. "Make lucky break, hah?"

Phil chuckled, slapping Oskar on the back. "You're a pretty smart fella, Oskar—I've gotta hand it to you. Just be careful, okay?"

Hmm. I wondered what *that* was about. I wanted to stick around to find out more, but I figured I'd better keep after Mr. Applegate. I had to run to catch up to him, but I finally caught sight of him, heading for the door to the parking deck.

I waited till the door closed behind him, and a good ten seconds more, before heading over there. I was determined to follow him all the way to his car—just in case he made another call.

But before I got to the door, I heard a loud commotion coming from behind me. I ducked into the alcove in front of a store entrance before anyone saw me.

There were several voices, all of them shouting. Most sounded like kids my age—but the loudest of all belonged to Oskar, no doubt about it. He was roaring in what sounded like part English, part foreign language.

"Get out from this place, you hoodlums! Don't come here no more! You are the bad news! Go away now, you hear?"

Taking a peek, I saw the group of kids who'd

confessed to doing the spray-painting. They were backing away from Oskar, their hands spread out in front of them, palms open, saying, "What? What did we do? We've got a right to be here."

Well, it was after closing time, so technically, they didn't—but I knew where they were coming from. I know how it feels to have adults chase you away from every good hangout spot. Sometimes kids get too loud, okay. But most times, it's just out of meanness that they hassle you.

And Oskar was mean, no doubt about it. Mean and *shifty*.

The group of teens was backing right up to where I was hiding. I flattened myself against the wall and turned my back, hiding my head in my jacket to make myself less visible.

Luckily, the kids' attention was on Oskar, and his attention was on them. No one noticed me cowering there. A good thing, too—it would have been really embarrassing to get caught like that.

I heard the door to the parking deck open, then slam shut. Oskar shouted, "And you stay out! No come back tomorrow—no come back *never*!"

He shuffled back past the entryway where I was huddled, but again, he didn't see me. His eyes were focused on something inside his head, and he was muttering to himself. "Stupid kids . . . get throw in jail, or worser! Why they no get job, make money, be like normal people? Crazy . . ."

I wanted to follow him and see where he went—but first, I needed to make sure those kids were really gone. I tiptoed over to the parking deck door and tried to open it without making any sound.

It wasn't hard, because the door lock was taped over with duct tape. Obviously, someone wanted to make sure they weren't locked out of the mall tonight.

I lingered there for a minute, deciding whether to pull off the tape. It wasn't an easy call. On the one hand, if I let a criminal back in and they got away with something bad, it would be my fault. On the other hand, if Frank and I expected to catch someone in the act, we *had* to let them back in!

Oskar had almost disappeared from my line of sight. I decided to follow him without removing the tape from the door. Just then, I caught a quick glimpse of someone else, dashing across the promenade and into a side corridor. Someone female, blond, with braids, a headband, and dangling earrings.

It had to be Frank's new boss. She was out on bail, but I knew the police would have warned her to stay away from the scene of her alleged crime. Meaning *here*—which would put her in danger of being hauled off to jail if she were caught.

Was she stalking Applegate? If she was the one he was talking to on the phone, it was possible. But I thought it was more likely Oskar she was interested in. He'd just told Phil he was going to be rich—and it seemed to me that he wasn't talking about a lottery ticket.

If he had picked something out of the glass that night—and Frank swore he had—it might have been something that fell from the roof along with the glass. Something that could identify the person who made it fall . . .

Perfect *blackmail* material.

I wondered if Steph had seen me. I didn't think so, because she'd been looking in Oskar's direction while she crossed the promenade.

Oskar himself was out of sight now, hidden by the fountain and the pool that surrounded it. I checked the side corridor, but Steph had disappeared. There were two doors, and I tried them both. Locked—surprise, surprise.

I wondered if she would have had a key—and if so, how she'd gotten it. Or maybe I'd just gone down the wrong corridor. . . .

Suddenly I heard a man cry out in pain—and then a loud *splash*!

Forgetting about Steph, I ran back down the

promenade. I was about ten feet short of the fountain when I stopped in my tracks. My heart was thumping so hard in my chest that I thought it would leap right out through my rib cage.

Something was floating facedown in the wishing pool.

No, not something—someone!

As I watched in horror, the body, moved by the current of the bubbling fountain, slowly turned over.

It was Oskar—and he was very, very dead.

10.
We Get a Clue

It had been a slow evening, and my legs were starting to get cramped. I'd been crouching behind this potted palm tree for what seemed like forever.

The mall after closing time was a very quiet place. A lone security man made his rounds every fifteen minutes or so, but that was it. In a more modern mall, there'd have been security cameras everywhere, and men in a video booth *watching* the monitors. But not here at good old East Side.

Nothing much else was happening in my sector. I found myself wondering how Joe was making out.

Then suddenly I heard a loud cry of pain and a splash from the direction of the fountain. That was enough to get me out of my hiding place in a hurry!

When I got to the fountain, Joe was already up to his knees in the water, dragging Oskar toward me.

Oskar didn't look too good.

"Joe! What happened?"

"What does it look like? Come on, Frank, give me a hand here—this guy weighs a ton!"

"Corpses usually do," I said, taking off my shoes and socks and rolling up my pants before getting into the pool.

"Gee, take your time," Joe commented.

"Hey, give me a break. He's already dead, the poor old guy—I mean, he was kind of nasty, but he sure didn't deserve *this*."

We laid Oskar down on the floor. That's when I saw the huge lump on the back of his head. "Looks like somebody conked him with something."

I checked in the pool. Sure enough, there was a large lava lamp resting on the bottom. I fished it out and showed it to Joe. The price tag read In the Groove.

"I saw a blond lady running around here just before it happened," Joe said. "She had long braids with a headband, and torn jeans. . . . I'm pretty sure it was Steph."

"Sounds like her, all right."

"I guess it looks *really* bad for her now, huh?"

"Like it didn't before? You know, I think it's very

120

possible somebody *wants* it to look that way."

"Come to think of it, it could have been that gang of kids," Joe said. "Someone taped up the door to the parking garage so they could come back in. It might have been the kids."

"Did you see them?"

"No. I was following the blonde."

"Hmm. That's my brother—always going after the ladies."

"Hey, can it, okay? Steph was acting very suspicious."

"Well, she's not supposed to be hanging around here at all, according to the conditions of her bail," I said.

"I know—that's what I mean!" He told me about overhearing Applegate's two phone conversations, and his suspicion that the first was with Steph. "He gave her a twenty-four-hour deadline for *something*, Frank. Maybe she got desperate. She sure was acting that way."

"It might not have been her he was talking to," I pointed out. "Meanwhile, how do you know it was those kids who taped the door? Maybe it was Steph."

"No way, Frank. As a store owner, she would've had a key."

I looked back over at the fountain. "Hey, Joe,"

I said, noticing something I hadn't seen before. "Check this out—over here."

On the bottom of the pool, near where Oskar had been floating, the coins people had thrown into the fountain had been arranged in a distinct pattern: STEMM. And this time, the Ms were interlocking.

Joe gave me a look.

"It's not proof of anything," I said. "Those kids tried to make her look guilty once before, remember?"

Oskar's broom/rake, fitted with mesh to scoop up the coins for collection, was still floating on the water. I fished it out but left the coins there for the police to find. After all, it was about time we called them.

Chief Collig was all over me and Joe. He grilled us like a pair of hot dogs—no, make that Phil's Phranks. And from what we told him, he quickly decided on a course of action.

"This has gone far enough," he told Con Reilly and the other senior officers standing by his side. "We're talkin' murder now. I want that woman taken in—and this time, for keeps. And drag that bunch of no-good kids in while you're at it—no sense taking chances."

The press were gathered outside, flashbulbs popping, trying to get a few pictures through the glass of the doors. "I've got to get out there and make a statement to those vultures," the chief muttered to Reilly. "Think you can handle things in here for a while?"

"No problem, Chief," said Con.

"I won't be too long."

After he was gone, I turned to Joe and said, "I don't believe Paul Burns and those kids killed Oskar. Do you?"

"There was bad blood between them, Frank—you saw how they kept bothering him."

"Yeah, but that's not the same thing as *killing* him."

"What if he threatened them or something?"

"Joe, he was killed with a *lava lamp*—one that still had a price tag on it. Someone obviously was thinking ahead enough to walk into In the Groove and grab it off the shelf, knowing in advance that they were going to smash it over Oskar's head. I don't think those kids are capable of that much planning."

"Good point," he had to admit. "But the fact remains that the lamp came from In the Groove. It's the kind of store those kids would shop at. So maybe one of them ducked in, grabbed it on the spur of the moment, and conked Oskar."

I shook my head. "I don't buy it."

"Well, then, maybe we're trying to make this whole thing more complicated than it is. Maybe Stephanie Flowers killed him after all. Maybe it was part of STEMM's sabotage campaign."

Maybe, but somehow, it just didn't sit right.

"Why would they kill Oskar as part of a sabotage campaign?" I asked. "Wouldn't they just try to do damage to the property itself? And besides, the warning said 'Next time during business hours.' If you believe it came from STEMM, then Oskar's murder makes no sense."

"Wait a second!" Joe cried, smacking himself in the forehead. "I forgot to tell you. I overheard Oskar telling Phil that he was going to be rich. It wasn't ten minutes before he died."

I grabbed him by both shoulders. "Joe, don't you remember the night the glass fell, I caught Oskar picking something out of the shattered glass and hiding it in his pocket? I chased after him, but he must have hidden it someplace before I caught up with him."

"Yeah, I remember. What ever happened with that?"

"What if Oskar found a piece of incriminating

evidence pointing to whoever cut the glass? If he tried to blackmail that person . . ."

"Of course!" Joe spoke excitedly. "But what *was* it? And where is it now?"

"Whoever killed Oskar probably has it," I said. "Unless . . ."

"Unless what?"

"Unless Oskar was keeping it safe . . . in which case, it might still be wherever he hid it that night! Come on, Joe. Follow me!"

I led him away from the fountain, all the way down the promenade to that little corridor where I'd cornered Oskar. "If he didn't come back for it, it has to be in one of these two rooms."

Fishing my lock-picking set out of my pocket, I got to work on the first of the two doors. It opened pretty easily. Inside was a broom closet—an empty one at that. It took us all of three minutes to scour it and move on.

The second room was also a closet—but this one held Oskar's spare overalls, coat, and hat. I checked all the pockets. There was some change, a dirty hankie—and a sleek, slim, tiny, very expensive-looking cell phone—one that could never in a million years have belonged to Oskar.

"Hey, Joe—check this out."

"Whoa! Pay dirt!" he said, recognizing it instantly as an important clue. "Well, fire it up, bro! Let's find out whose it is!"

I hit the on button, but nothing happened. "Hmm. Battery must be dead." I checked the charger input—it was tiny. We were definitely going to need a special charger—something we couldn't get till morning.

"I guess we'll just have to wait," said Joe, pocketing it.

"Hey, who found it?" I asked, sticking my hand out.

"Oh, all right," he said, handing it over. "Baby's gotta have his toy."

11.
The Big Chill

That night Frank and I did an Internet search to find out who'd posted Stephanie Flowers's bail. There were about six hundred AA Associates listed, and after the first seventy-five or so, we were getting mighty bleary-eyed.

"This is going to take all night," I complained. "I need my beauty sleep."

"It might be important, Joe," Frank said, struggling to keep his own eyes open. "You go ahead and catch a few z's. I'll keep this going."

"Yeah, until you conk out on the keyboard."

He laughed. "Bound to happen pretty soon," he agreed.

I proceeded to nod off. I dreamed that I was about to corner Oskar's killer. I had them backed up

127

against a wall. Slowly they turned . . . and it was—

Frank shook me awake. "Joe!" he said. "Joe, wake up!"

"Aw, man—I was just about to reveal his identity!"

"Huh?"

"Never mind. What's all the commotion about?"

"I hit pay dirt, Joe. A certain AA Associates is listed for Freeport, the Bahamas, and one of its officers is an A. Applegate!"

"Mr. Applegate? From the mall?"

"Do you know his first name?" he asked.

"I think it's Arthur, right?"

"Arthur starts with an *A*, Joe."

"Okay, but why would he bail Steph out?"

"I don't know, but tomorrow we're going to go find out."

"Uh, what about school, dude?"

He shrugged and sighed. "Ah, you know, tomorrow's just going to be one of those days. We'll skip out after lunch. We'll have to get a note from Dr. ATAC saying we had an appointment, and make up the classwork after the case is wrapped."

Next afternoon we left during lunch. We waved at Iola and Chet, who were hanging out by the front gate reading a newspaper.

Oh, well. We'd have to fill them in later. I was sure they had a pretty good idea of what we were up to, anyway. They don't know we're in ATAC, of course—but they do know we're amateur detectives, and that we sometimes skip school when we're hot on a case.

The paper Iola and Chet were reading was all about the murder at the East Side Mall. We'd seen it on our doorstep and given it a quick look—enough to know that Bayport's mayor and town council had already discussed closing the East Side Mall down until further notice. Their decision was due by the end of the day.

Frank and I headed over to North Bay Boulevard, where there was a store specializing in upscale cell phones and equipment of a certain brand. We bought a car charger and plugged it into the outlet on Frank's bike.

He hit the on button, and the little high-tech wonder sprang to life. Blue light flickered along its edges, a rainbow of colors lit up its high-def display, and an awesome microspeaker blasted out the theme from Beethoven's Fifth Symphony.

"Wow," Frank said. "I've got to get me one of those. You think we could hit up ATAC for a couple of these babies?"

"You know, that's a good idea—"

Suddenly the phone started to vibrate in Frank's hand.

Someone was calling!

"Hello?" He listened for a minute, and his eyes lit up. "No, it isn't. He, uh, left it with me by mistake, but I'll make sure he gets the message. Who is this again? Ned Lerner, from the Bar Association, about his annual donation? Yes, I'll tell him. Thank you."

He flipped the phone shut and grinned at me excitedly. "This phone belongs to Bob Meister!"

"I knew it," I said. "He's the one who paid those kids to spray that graffiti, and he planted the lava lamp in the fountain."

"Paul Burns must have lied to me when he said Steph paid him," said Frank, thinking back. "Remember I told you that when I first asked who paid him, he said some things were worse than going to prison? I guess he was scared enough of Meister to lie about it."

"Based on what happened to Oskar, I guess the kid was right to be scared," I said. "This phone must have dropped out of Meister's pocket while he was up there cutting the skylight—"

"And then Oskar found it," Frank finished. "He must have tried to blackmail Meister—a dangerous game."

"You know what, Frank?" I said. "It all makes sense! Meister would have every reason to damage the mall's reputation and blame it on STEMM. If he succeeded, the town might close the mall down as a safety hazard. Applegate would lose so much money he'd be forced to sell, and Shangri-La could swoop in and buy it for less!"

"Except Meister had to go and lose his phone," Frank put in. "A bad mistake—which Oskar planned to make him pay for."

"Which is why Meister had to kill him. And he used the lava lamp to implicate Steph, the way he's done with everything else!"

"I agree. I think we've got our killer, Joe. Now all we have to do is prove it."

"Prove it? What about the cell phone?"

"Funny thing is, it probably wouldn't have stood up as evidence in court. But I guess Meister wasn't about to take that chance."

"So what do we do now?"

Frank blew out a long breath. "I guess we start by tracking him down."

"No problem!" I said, feeling much better. "That's always my favorite part of a case."

Our first stop was Shangri-La Enterprises, just a few blocks away. We rode over there, parked our bikes around the corner, and walked to the building's front entrance.

"I'll provide a diversion for you at the front desk," I told Frank. "You just go on through and up to the thirty-fourth floor."

"Why me?" Frank asked. "You've already been there!"

"*Exactly*. They all know me—the lobby security guys, Eberhardt, Meister, their secretaries. After the stunts I pulled last time, I'd have zero chance of getting through."

So that was how it went down. I went straight up to the lobby security desk and asked to see Mr. Eberhardt. When the guard told me I needed an appointment, I started arguing with him.

Meanwhile, I had cleverly positioned myself so that the guard had his back to Frank—who walked right on through to the elevators, totally unnoticed.

As soon as he'd disappeared inside one of them, I gave up the fight and apologized to the guard. "I'm sorry," I said. "I had no right to get angry with you—I mean, you're just doing your job, right?"

"Right," the guy said, sounding relieved and a little puzzled. A minute ago I'd been acting angry enough to cause bodily harm. Now, without any help from him, I was suddenly a pussycat.

I waited outside the building, sitting on the

front steps, out of the way of foot traffic, until Frank came out five minutes later.

"Well?" I asked.

"Well," he said, sitting down next to me, "I went up to thirty-four and told the receptionist I had a personal message to deliver to Mr. Meister, from Mr. Lerner of the American Bar Association."

"And?"

"She said, 'I'll have to give him the message—he called in sick this morning.' I gave her a look like I didn't believe her, and then she said, 'No, really, he did. He sounded just awful, too—his voice was practically gone.'"

"Hmm . . . or maybe it wasn't him at all!"

"That occurred to me, too, Joe. But why would someone do that? Why wouldn't Meister just call in sick himself?"

I shrugged. "I don't have a clue, Sherlock. How about you?"

He shook his head. "If Meister killed Oskar, he'd probably want to lay low until he was sure it was safe to show himself."

"So how do we find him?"

"How 'bout we try dialing information?"

Frank couldn't get his address from the operator, but we did find it in one of the phone books at the Bayport Public Library.

We rode over there—way over into the suburbs north of town along the bay. Meister lived in a nice house, all right—but from the looks of things, he wasn't home. No car in the driveway or the garage, no sign of life inside.

We checked in by phone with police headquarters next. Con Reilly answered. He told me they were still searching for Stephanie Flowers, but that they'd rounded up Paul Burns and his friends and were grilling them for information about Oskar's murder.

"Can I suggest something, Con?" I asked.

"Sure."

"Tell them you know the truth about who paid them to spray that graffiti."

He sounded surprised. "*They're* the ones who did that? How'd you find that out?"

"Frank wormed it out of them, but they lied about who paid them."

"But you think they'll tell *us* the truth."

"Well, yeah. If they tell you it was Stephanie Flowers, don't believe it."

"Oh, no? Why not?"

"Just trust me on this one, Con. If they say it was her, tell them you know it wasn't. Tell them you know it was Bob Meister."

"Bob who?"

"He's the lawyer for Shangri-La Enterprises, LLC."

"Are you nuts, Joe? Shangri-La is a major player in this city. I'm not going to start dragging their name into this mess, and neither is the chief!"

"Just try it, Con, okay? You might be surprised at their reaction."

He sighed. "All right. But I expect a full explanation later."

"No problem," I said. "You'll have it by the end of the day." I flipped my phone shut. "At least, I sure hope so."

We headed over to the mall next. We weren't due at work for another hour, but we couldn't think of a better place to look for Meister.

I didn't buy for one second that he was really sick. He hadn't gotten his cell phone back, after all. He might still be looking for it, and the mall was one place Oskar could have hidden it (I'd have bet Oskar's apartment had already been searched).

Frank headed for In the Groove first, to see if Adriana had shown up. I made a beeline for the food court.

Clem was behind the counter at Healthy Wraps. "I can't believe it—you're early!" he greeted me.

"Oh, no. I don't start for another hour."

He shook his head and frowned. "I don't know.

First you don't show up, then you show up early, but not to work . . . ."

"Just remember, Clem—the price is right," I said.

"Well, salary or no salary—you'd better be here in an hour, ready to work, or the whole deal's off!"

"All righty, then." I was ready to lose the job anyway, now that the case had completely taken over my life. Besides, Clem was turning out to be a real pain.

I took a seat at a table, not far from Phil's Phranks 'n' Phries. At this early hour, not even Phil's was busy. In fact, only one place was doing any business at all: The Big Chill.

Chet was behind the counter, scooping up enormous portions to a crowd of juniors from Bayport High. I recognized a few of them: Sam Scarfone, Adam Franklin, the Daniels twins, Tommy Carroll . . .

Suddenly there was a commotion as Chet's boss Ernesto arrived and saw what was going on. You'd think he'd have been happy about all those customers, but no.

"What kind of portions are you giving out?" he screamed at Chet. "You want to send me to the poorhouse? Look—*this* is how you do it!"

He grabbed the scoop from Chet and handled the next customer himself. She gave him a nasty look when she saw how small her cone was, compared to all the ones Chet had doled out.

"Hey!" she said, frowning. "This place is a rip-off!"

"You see what you're doing to me?" the boss shouted at Chet. "And look—now we're out of vanilla! Go back in the freezer and get me some more!"

He turned to argue with the angry girl, while Chet disappeared into the storage area in back of the food stalls.

A minute later I heard him *screaming*.

I stood up and turned to look, just like everyone else. Chet stepped out of the storage area, empty-handed. In fact, he was waving his hands around like they were on fire. "HELP! Somebody help!!"

Everyone else seemed frozen, so I sprang into action, leaping over the counter and sprinting to his side. "What's up, Chet? What's wrong?"

"Th-th-there's a d-dead man in there!" he stammered, pointing behind him.

I let go of him and rushed back to the storage area. The door to the food court's walk-in freezer was wide open, and a cold mist was pouring out of it. I waved it away as I went inside.

And that's when I saw *him*.

At the back of the freezer, sitting on a pile made of cases of Phil's Phranks, was the frozen body of our number one suspect—Bob Meister!

12.
A Friend in Need

When I got there, In the Groove was still locked up. Adriana was nowhere in sight, and neither was Steph. In fact, my boss hadn't been seen since just before Oskar's murder. The police hadn't been able to find her, and neither had anyone else.

So where was she? Had she skipped town? Left the state—the country, even?

I didn't think so. Something told me Stephanie Flowers was still close by. I didn't have any evidence—just the fact that she'd been here last night, and the logic that said she wasn't about to walk away from something she cared so much about.

Maybe she was just hiding, waiting until the police found the person who was really responsible for all this madness.

I was still standing there when I heard something that sounded like Chet Morton screaming "Help!" I took off at full speed for the food court, and arrived to find a huge crowd hanging around the Big Chill.

As I cut through the ranks of the curious, I could see that Chet was at the center of all the commotion. He was sitting on a high stool, looking distinctly green, with his boss at one shoulder and Iola at the other.

"Is he okay?" I called to Iola.

She shook her head. "But he'll live. Which is more than you can say for whoever's in there."

She nodded with her head toward an open door at the back of the food stand. Joe was standing in the doorway, motioning for me to join him.

As I passed Iola, she said, "Frank, when you've got a minute, I have to talk to you about something— something important."

"You want to tell me now?" I asked.

"No, later . . . in private."

She looked troubled—even worried. I wondered why, but Joe was hissing at me, waving for me to hurry up.

"Back here," he said. "In the freezer room."

I followed him in there—and that's when I saw the corpse. I didn't recognize the poor guy, but then, he was kind of blue, and probably not looking his best. "Do I know him?" I asked Joe.

"It's Meister. Looks like he's been in here awhile, too—maybe since last night. We should find out if anyone else came in here today."

"We should call the police, too."

"Already did," Joe said. "They're on their way."

"Joe, if Meister was in here since last night . . . he might not have been alive long enough to kill Oskar."

"Or maybe Oskar killed *him*, and then someone else killed *Oskar*."

"Who? Steph?"

"I'll tell you one thing—it wasn't Paul Burns and those kids, Frank. I would've heard them. Whoever killed Oskar did it solo, and quietly."

Chief Collig, Con Reilly, and two other officers burst into the freezer room.

"Great Caesar's ghost!" the chief cried when he saw Meister sitting there. Then he took a long look at the two of us. "All right, boys," he said, frowning. "Let's have it—the whole story, if you please—and don't leave anything out."

We started to tell him, and we were about halfway through when Reilly said, "Hey, chief—check this out." He handed the chief a folded piece of paper. "It was in the stiff's suit pocket."

The chief read it, looked up at us, and said, "It's a suicide note."

"No way!" Joe told him.

"I agree," I said. "No way."

The forensics officer joined our little group.

"How long has he been dead?" the chief asked her.

"Hard to tell, Chief, because the body's frozen," she said. "But not more than twelve hours."

The chief checked his watch. "That means he was killed sometime after three in the morning," he said. "Which means the janitor died first." He turned to us, looking grimmer than ever. "Finish your story, boys." And we did.

"Well, now, try this on for size," he said when we were done. "Meister here pays those juvenile delinquents to spray the graffiti on the roof to implicate STEMM. He cuts the glass and loses his cell phone. Oskar finds it and tries to blackmail him. He fights with Oskar and kills him. Then, out of guilt and remorse, Meister takes his own life."

"Chief, I don't want to sound rude, but that's absurd," I said.

"I think so too," said the chief, taking me by surprise. "And who would choose to die by freezing himself to death? That's a pretty extreme suicide."

"I think someone else wrote it, lured Meister in here, knocked him unconscious, then stuck the note in his pocket to make it *look* like suicide."

"There's just one problem," Chief Collig pointed out. "This freezer has a safety door—it can be opened from inside as well as out, so why didn't he let himself back out when he came to?"

"Well, then, maybe whoever lured Meister here killed him," I said. "It wouldn't have mattered that the door could be opened from in here, because Meister was already dead."

"Any evidence of violence on the body?" Chief Collig asked the forensics lady.

"No, sir."

"Well, have some toxicology tests run. The whole gamut. This man may have been poisoned." He turned to me and Frank. "All right, you two can go now. We'll take it from here."

"Chief?" Joe said.

"Go on now, it's freezing in here. Get some hot cocoa and thaw yourselves out—let the pros handle this. We're closing the mall and making everyone clear out."

Joe and I always hate when he does that—rubbing it in about us being amateurs. But we couldn't argue with him—not without revealing our secret

142

to every officer in that freezer room.

"Chief, one last thing," said Joe. "Could you show that note to my brother?"

The chief made a face, but handed me the note.

"Frank," Joe said. "You're a handwriting expert, right? Quick—tell me, was that note written by a righty or a lefty?"

One quick glance at the note was enough. "A righty," I stated. "Definitely."

"See, that *proves* it's not a suicide note. I've met Meister. I've seen him sign his name," said Joe, with a grim look on his face. "He was a lefty."

Chief Collig looked startled. "You're sure?"

"I'd testify to it in court."

"Well, then," said the chief. "I guess we've got *two* murders on our hands."

"What about suspects?" I asked. I didn't think the chief would answer, but I figured I'd try asking anyway.

To my surprise, he turned to Con Reilly and ordered, "Send out an all-points bulletin. I want Stephanie Flowers brought in—tonight!" Turning back to me and Joe, he added, "It can't be those kids. I've had them in custody since midnight on suspicion of the other murder."

"Are you going to let them go now?" Joe asked.

"No way," the chief said, shaking his head. "Just because they didn't kill our frozen fish here doesn't mean they didn't drown the janitor. Until we speak to Ms. Flowers and get a full confession, they stay locked up."

Thoughts and theories were racing through my head, but I wasn't clear enough about them to lay it out for Chief Collig. I needed some time to toss things around with Joe and put the whole case together in my mind. "Come on, Joe," I said. "I'm freezing."

We went back out into the food court, where it felt like a hundred degrees by comparison. A team of paramedics with a stretcher marched past us toward the freezer, but Joe and I knew there wasn't any hurry. Meister was gone—and with him, our number one suspect.

Which left only Steph, really, if you didn't count those kids—and I was satisfied they weren't killers. Trouble was, I didn't think Steph was either. . . .

Chet came over to us, still looking a little green. "I can't believe what just happened!" he said, his voice shaking.

"Calm down, buddy," Joe told him.

"Hey, where's Iola?" I asked Chet, remembering that she wanted to tell me something.

"Uh, I guess she went home."

"No, she wouldn't have done that." I looked

around some more, craning my neck to see past the crowd of shoppers that had gathered to watch this bizarre *CSI: Bayport* reality show, live from the food court.

Iola was nowhere in sight. *Strange*, I thought.

There was her boss behind the counter, closing up for the night. "Excuse me, Phil," I said, going up to him. "Is Iola around?"

"Iola? Uh, no, she must have taken off."

"She was just here a few minutes ago."

"Yeah, but in all the commotion . . ."

"She didn't tell you she was leaving?"

"No, but like I said, everyone was watching the—well, you know . . ."

"Yeah. So, you didn't see her leave, then?"

"No. She might still be around somewhere. Maybe in the bathroom?"

"Okay, thanks anyway."

I stood at the entrance to the ladies' room and shouted Iola's name. There was no response, so I went back over to Joe and Chet. "You sure you didn't see her go?" I asked Chet.

He shook his head. "I was distracted! But don't worry—I'm sure she just went home, Frank."

"She said she needed to talk to me," I told him. "She looked scared, but it was just after the body was found. I told her to wait for me, Chet—she wouldn't have just left." The alarm bells going off in my head suddenly got a whole lot louder. "We should go look for her. *Now*."

"Should we split up?" Joe asked.

"Good idea. I'll go that way, toward In the Groove. Joe, you go toward Applegate's office. Chet, you head thataway. If none of us finds her, there's only one direction left—toward the parking deck. That's where she would have headed if she was leaving the mall—so once we do our search, we'll know she's not still here."

We took off at a jog, each of us searching a different promenade. We arrived back at the food court ten minutes later, empty-handed. Meanwhile, the body had been taken away, and the food court had been cleared of everyone but the police, who were finishing up their investigation.

"I want a twenty-four-hour police detail on this entire mall," the chief told Reilly.

"We're short of men, Chief. They're all out after that Flowers woman."

"Well, then, as soon as she's apprehended!"

Right on cue, we all heard screaming and shouting coming from the direction of the emergency stairs.

"Let me go! This is police brutality! The whole world is watching!"

It was Steph! She had her hands cuffed behind her back and was being marched down the promenade by a couple of big, burly police officers. Her hair was wild and uncombed, and she was struggling with every ounce of her strength, like some untamed animal.

I felt sorry for her, and I wasn't the only one. Mr. Applegate came running up behind the procession, yelling, "Let her go! Let her go—I'll take responsibility for her!"

"Sorry, Mr. A.," said Chief Collig. "This woman is wanted for two murders. I should think you, more than anybody, would want to see her in handcuffs."

"She's no murderer!" Mr. Applegate insisted. "She's . . . she's my granddaughter."

"She's your *what*?" exclaimed the chief.

"My granddaughter."

Mr. Applegate, who must have been around seventy-five in real life, looked about a hundred at that moment. Tears streamed down his cheeks as he hugged Steph, who was also crying her eyes out.

"I'm sorry to hear that, Pops," said Con Reilly as the police hauled Steph away, still protesting her innocence.

His granddaughter? No wonder he'd bailed her out!

147

"We've been on . . . well, bad terms for the past year," Applegate explained as he dabbed at his eyes with a handkerchief. "Ever since I decided to retire and sell this place. Stephanie loved it so much, you see. She's loved it ever since she was a little girl . . . that's why she opened her store here. And she loved that marsh, too. Maybe she loved it too much."

He sniffed back tears, moaning, "But she couldn't have done what they say she did! She *couldn't* have—I *know* her! She cares too much about people to harm anyone—why, she even cares about endangered insects!"

I was inclined to agree about Steph—but there was no time to stay and console him. "Joe," I said. "We've got to find Iola—and fast!"

"Right."

"Chet, you stay here. If Iola shows up, call one of us on the cell."

"Okay, but what's wrong?"

"We'll tell you later," I said, already heading for the parking deck.

We couldn't go *too* fast—we had to check every nook and cranny along the way, just to make sure she wasn't still here—but I was afraid we were already too late. If Iola had seen something, or someone, related to the murder of Bob Meister, she was in grave danger.

The parking deck was virtually empty—a stray car here and there, but it was pretty clear that we were the only ones around.

"What now?" asked Joe.

"Let's get to our bikes and drive around the local streets—see if we can spot something," I said, feeling more worried than ever.

We went up to the third level, where our motorcycles were parked. We were just about to kick them into gear when we heard a bloodcurdling scream!

It came from above us, up on the roof of the parking deck.

"Help! Help me, somebody!"

Iola!

Joe and I were already running full speed, and we're pretty fast. But you know how parking decks are—you have to go around in circles as you climb the levels. We listened as we ran, but we heard no more screams, no more cries for help.

We finally made it up there, and paused to catch our breath and look around. The roof of the deck was empty—*almost.*

There was only one car—Iola's. It was parked in the outside row, with its front end facing the guardrail.

Even from where I stood, directly across the

rooftop deck, I could tell that the rail had been pried loose. It wasn't totally broken through, but enough so that it wouldn't offer much protection.

The car's motor was running, and its front bumper was right up against the loosened rail. Just a little pressure on the accelerator, and . . .

I could see Iola, sitting in the front passenger seat. Her mouth was gagged (no wonder she'd stopped screaming!) and her eyes were wide with terror. I had to assume her hands and feet were tied too—although I couldn't see them.

On the driver's side, someone was standing outside the car, leaning through the open window—probably saying something to Iola.

Then he stood up.

The parking deck's lights were off, but in the moonlight on the roof, I could see his silvery hair. I could also see the silver pistol in his right hand as he swung it away from Iola and leveled it at us.

"I advise you not to move," he said in a calm, deep voice.

I couldn't make out his facial features from this far away, but I didn't need to. I knew exactly who it was—who it *had* to be.

13.
Big-Time Evil

"Ralph Eberhardt!" I gasped.

"Guilty as charged," he said, walking slowly toward us with his gun swinging back and forth between Frank and me. "Well, well, if it isn't young Mr. Hardy, son of the famous Fenton. I'm guessing this would be your brother?"

"You killed Meister, didn't you," Frank said, his hands held high over his head. It was a statement, not a question.

"Never mind about that," said Eberhardt as he moved around behind us. "Just walk slowly toward the car—and don't try anything foolish."

"You were the one behind this whole thing, right from the beginning, weren't you?" Frank told him. "From the e-mails that supposedly came from STEMM, to the falling skylight, to the murders of Oskar and Meister."

"You're wrong about almost everything, young man," Eberhardt said as we reached the car. "Now, turn around and face me."

We did. I could see the gun now. It was a .38 caliber revolver—big and bad enough to blow some nasty holes in us. I gave Frank a quick look and saw that he was thinking the same thing. No use trying to jump Eberhardt with that thing in his hand—one of us was bound to get killed in the process.

Eberhardt grabbed a roll of duct tape that was sitting on the hood of the car and tossed it to me. "All right, now tape your brother's wrists and ankles together."

What choice did I have? I started with the ankles, trying not to tape them too tightly. Then I proceeded to work on Frank's wrists.

"Not that way—behind his back!" Eberhardt ordered.

When I was finished, he ordered me to step away from the car. Then he opened the car door and shoved Frank into the backseat. Turning to me, he said, "Now it's your turn."

He motioned me over to the other side of the vehicle, then ordered me to put my hands behind my back. "I've got the gun in one hand," he told me as he used the other to tape my wrists.

Knowing he was doing it with just one hand, I kept my wrists slightly separated. Later on, that might give me a chance to work them free.

"All right, sit down in the back and stick your ankles out." I did, and he taped them together before slamming the door on me. Then he leaned in through the open front window. "There. I think that just about does it."

Iola made a sobbing noise, and Eberhardt sighed, shaking his head. "I'm sorry to have to do this, young lady. I'm not a violent man by nature, but you kids just couldn't keep your noses out of my business, could you?"

"It's not just your business—not when you're endangering other people's lives," Frank said through gritted teeth.

"It didn't have to go that far," said Eberhardt, stuffing the gun back into his belt now that he no longer needed it. "I never intended for anyone to get hurt. But that old fool Applegate didn't know a good deal when he saw one."

"What part of his saying no didn't you understand?" I asked.

"I don't *take* no for an answer, young man. If I did, I wouldn't be the wildly successful businessman I am."

"So you decided to sabotage the mall in order to force Applegate to sell," Frank said.

"Sabotage? Oh, not me! I'm not someone who likes to get his own hands dirty. That's why I had Bob Meister working for me." He laughed. "Do you know, we used to call him the Hammer, because he was so tough. Too bad he got a bit out of control, and I had to bring the hammer down on him."

"What do you mean?" I asked.

"He made some stupid mistakes—mistakes that threatened to leave a trail leading right back to Shangri-La, and to yours truly. I felt pretty safe with the Bayport police on the case, but when *you* showed up at my office that day, Joe, I knew I would have to step in personally and take care of business."

"Did you kill Oskar?" Frank asked him.

"Oh, no. That was Bob. I understand the janitor found his cell phone amid the glass debris, realized Bob had to have been up on the roof, and threatened to expose him to the police if he wasn't paid an outrageous sum of money."

Again Eberhardt laughed, showing his perfect white teeth. "Well, Bob was quite a cheapskate, you know. He didn't like to be taken advantage of. And, as I said, we didn't call him the Hammer for nothing."

"So he killed Oskar, and then *you* killed *him*?" I asked.

"Yes I did, if you must know. Not personally, of course. As I told you, I don't like getting dirty. But I *had* to do something. Bob's mistakes were ruining my whole business strategy."

"So you had an inside man at the mall the whole time!" declared Frank.

Eberhardt flashed Frank an icy smile. "Bravo, Fenton Junior. Right after he killed the janitor, Bob called me. He was still at the mall, lying low until the police got through poking around. I realized right then that something had to be done, so I got in touch with my 'inside man,' as you call him. Luckily, he was still there. He found Meister and told Bob he'd better hide in the freezer until it was safe."

"What happened then?"

"Oh, he gave Bob a little injection. A lethal one. I suppose the police will eventually figure that part out—but it will never be traced back to me, or to my 'inside man,' either. Not once you're taken care of."

Eberhardt backed away from the car and stood up. "Ah, there you are! It's about time you made it," he said, looking off into the distance at an approaching figure—one I thought I recognized. . . .

Yes! It was him, all right—Phil, of Phil's Phranks 'n' Phries!

"Hello, everybody!" Phil said, grinning at the three of us. "Goin' for a little ride?"

"He told me he didn't know where Iola was!" Frank muttered.

"Sorry. I lied." Phil shrugged. "See, your girlfriend opened the wrong drawer and found my hypodermic." He drew a Tech-9 out of his belt. "Lucky thing I don't keep *this* in the drawer. That's how I persuaded her to come up here, where Mr. Eberhardt was waiting."

"*Why*, Phil?" I asked him. "You've got a good business—why would you risk it all to get involved in a scheme like this?"

"A very good question," Eberhardt said, beaming. "You've got a good head for business, Joe—too bad you'll never get to use it. But you're right. Why don't you tell him what's in it for you, Phil?"

"I've always imagined going global," said Phil, a dreamy look on his face. "Can you imagine? An international chain of Phil's Phranks 'n' Phries, with outlets at every mall in the country!"

I had to roll my eyes. I mean, Phil's Phries are really, really good, it's true—but the Phranks? *Heartburn city*.

"And now," said Eberhardt, "I'm afraid our time—or rather, yours—is up."

"What are you going to do?" Frank asked.

"Don't you know?" Eberhardt answered. "You're a bright boy—figure it out."

156

"I know you're going to kill us," said Frank. "But how exactly?"

I knew he was buying more time and trying to get as much information as he could. It was the only chance we had left.

"If you lean forward, you can see that Phil here has rigged a very special contraption. He's extremely clever that way."

"Maybe he should make mousetraps instead of those awful Phranks," I said.

"Awful? Why, I oughta—" Phil raised the gun, ready to smash it across my face, but Eberhardt put a hand up to stop him.

"Please, Phil. No blood. I can't stand the sight of it. Let's get out of here and watch the fireworks from downstairs."

"Fine," said Phil, smirking at me. "I'll just light the fuse here. . . ."

He did, and it started to sputter and glow. He made a wiping-hands gesture. "It's a long way down, but it'll be over in two seconds," he told us. "You won't suffer, trust me."

Trust him? This guy was a moron *and* a maniac!

"Bon voyage," said Eberhardt. "I'm so sorry it had to end like this. But you know what they say— business is business."

14.
Over the Edge

I watched the fuse sputter to life. I looked at the whole length of it and figured we had—at most—two minutes to come up with a way out of this. After that, the fuse would reach the rope Phil had looped around the steering column. On the other end of that rope was a lead brick.

When the rope burned through, the brick would drop right onto the accelerator, sending the car straight into fourth gear and right through the weakened guardrail!

Luckily, Joe hadn't taped me too tightly. Still, duct tape is duct tape. It's sticky, and really hard to work free of, unlike plain old rope, which tends to give way when you work it back and forth.

"I . . . can't get . . . free of it!" Joe was muttering as he strained to work his own wrists free.

Iola was trying to say something, but the gag over her mouth made it come out as a groan of frustration. Her eyes were getting wider and wider, and I wished I could have helped her—but I couldn't even help myself!

Eberhardt had been smarter than us, right from the very beginning. Joe and I had been a step behind him all along—by the time we were onto Oskar, he was dead. Meister? Same story.

Eberhardt had burned each bridge behind him as he crossed it, so that the crimes he committed through others would never be traced back to him. Iola, Joe, and I were the last links between him and the unfortunate events at the East Side Mall—and soon, we too would be dead.

We'd never figured out that there had to be someone on the inside—someone at the mall all day and evening, watching what went on and reporting back to the boss.

Phil.

I watched as he and Eberhardt opened the door to the stairway and disappeared. I kept on racking my brain for a way out of this mess, but nothing was coming to me.

Joe's constant refrain of "Come on, Frank!"

didn't help either. And Iola's pleading eyes made it even worse.

"It's over, isn't it, Frank?" Joe suddenly said. His voice was calm. Not a trace of fear—just facing the truth. After all our narrow escapes and brushes with death, this time we were really done for.

And then, just when we were about to give in to the inevitable, someone shouted, *"Over there!"* and two familiar figures came running across the roof toward us.

"Chet!" I yelled, recognizing his hulking frame. But who was that with him? "Adriana?"

"Frank! Are you okay? What happened?"

"There's no time to explain," I said. "Got anything sharp?"

"Huh?"

"Something to cut with," Joe shouted.

"Um . . . well, my barrette has a serrated edge . . ."

"Try it!" I said, holding my wrists out behind my back so she could start sawing away. "Chet—get the fuse!"

"Fuse?" He looked at me blankly.

"In the front, under the steering wheel! Don't let it burn through that rope!"

"Rope?"

"Chet, there's no time to waste!" In fact, the fuse had almost reached the rope already.

Okay, time for plan B.

"Never mind, Chet—go around and grab the rear bumper, and hold on to it for all you're worth!"

Thank goodness he understood that part. He ran around to the back of the car. "Got it!" Adriana's barrette finally cut through the duct tape, and she started on Joe's wrists.

"Hold on, and don't let go, pal—if you do, we're toast!" I called to Chet.

"*There!*" said Adriana as Joe's hands came free.

"Get Iola out of the car, quick!" he told her as he pulled the tape off his ankles.

Adriana ran around the back of the car as Joe tried to climb over the seat to the front. But the fuse had already set the rope on fire!

Before Adriana could open the passenger door and let Iola out, the rope burned through, and the heavy brick dropped onto the accelerator.

The car lurched forward, hurling Joe back into the rear seat. Adriana screamed as our front bumper banged into the guardrail and split it in two.

"AAAARRRRRHHH!" Chet was letting out a mighty roar, but he wasn't letting go of the back bumper.

Man, all that strength training sure was coming in handy!

"Joe, quick!" I yelled.

But he didn't need prompting. As soon as he recovered from his tumble, he rolled over the seat into the front, yanked the brick off the accelerator, and tried to throw the gear shift into park.

Nothing happened.

"Aw, man, he jammed it!" Joe yelled. The brick might have been off the gas pedal, but the car was still in drive.

"Okay, just get me out of here!" I told him.

First he shoved Iola out the passenger door, which Adriana had opened. Then he came around back for me.

The car was creeping forward, an inch at a time. The front tires were almost at the edge of the roof! But every time it looked like they would go over, they inched back again as Chet exerted himself in the deadly game of tug-of-war.

"I . . . can't . . . hold . . . on . . . much . . . longer!" he grunted.

Joe reached in and grabbed me, yanking me free and clear of the car, just as Chet's amazing strength gave out.

The car lurched forward, tipped over, and disappeared. A second later we heard the crash, followed by a hellacious fireball that made it all the way to the roof.

We staggered back, Iola and Adriana screaming. I

held Adriana, and Joe grabbed Iola, to shield them from the heat and smoke.

"OW!" I heard Chet say. "My hands are killing me!"

"You okay?" I asked.

"I'm gonna have blisters."

"Dude, you saved us!" Joe said, clapping Chet on the back.

"Don't thank me—thank her," he replied, pointing to Adriana. "She dragged me up here, saying Iola was in trouble!"

"How did you know?" I asked her.

She sniffed back tears and managed a smile. "As I was coming in from the deck, I saw Phil and Iola coming up here, and I thought it was a little weird—like, why would he be bringing her up there? And she had this scared look on her face too."

She wiped away some more tears and continued. "So I went to find someone from security, and when I got to the food court, I found out about the guy in the freezer! And there was Chet, getting questioned by the police. So as soon as they were done with him, I asked him where you guys were, and he said you'd gone to the parking deck, trying to catch the murderer. So I just grabbed Chet and we ran up here as fast as we could!"

"Well, we're sure glad you did," said Joe, looking gratefully at Adriana and Chet. Then he said to Chet, "Dude, you've got to hook me up with that personal trainer of yours—that was an awesome display!"

Chet grinned proudly, patted his stomach, and said, "Two hundred pounds of solid muscle, yo."

"Hey, Joe," I said. "I think it's time we went after those two dirtbags, before they get away."

"You think we still have a chance to catch them?" he asked.

"They said they were going to stay and watch," I reminded him. "I guess they wanted to make sure the car came down as planned. Well, it did—which means they think they're safe now. So they won't be in any hurry."

"All righty, then," said Joe. "Let's go for a little ride!"

"Will you guys be okay from here?" I asked the others.

They all nodded.

"Be careful, Frank," Adriana pleaded. "You too, Joe."

"We will," I assured her. "Let's get moving, Joe—every second counts!"

15.
The Chase Is On

Frank and I made a beeline for our motorcycles and revved them up full tilt. We circled down to the exit, then stopped for a moment to look at the intense fire from the wreck of Iola's car.

"Which way do we go now?" I asked Frank.

He shrugged his shoulders. "Your guess is as good as mine."

But it turned out we didn't have to guess. Eberhardt must have really enjoyed watching what he thought was the three of us burning to a crisp—because just then, a sleek-looking black sedan with tinted windows that had been sitting across the street with its headlights off suddenly screeched away from the curb, burning rubber.

"That has to be them!" I yelled, and we flipped our visors back down for the chase.

They had a couple blocks' head start on us, and a V-8 engine to boot—but that wasn't going to be enough to outrun our rides, with their turbo-boosted engines and fine-tuned maneuverability. Those bikes of ours are as good as their riders—and all bragging aside, Frank and I are very, very good.

After a mile or so, they could see that we were gaining on them. The driver—I could only assume it was Eberhardt—flicked his lights on, veered hard to the right, and sped up Bigelow Boulevard, away from the bay and into Bayport proper.

We were after them in a flash, but it was harder keeping up with them here in town. The sedan kept making sudden turns, forcing us to overshoot and make quick wheelies.

Once or twice we thought we'd lost them altogether, only to spot them again as they came back around in a circle, trying to lose us but finding us instead.

Finally Frank motioned for me to stop. We pulled over, and he raised his visor. "Let's split up and circle around them," he said. "If we can get in front, we can zap them with the hot button!"

Boy, I liked that idea! It isn't often that we got to use any of the high-tech gadgetry ATAC packed into our bikes—and the hot button is one of my favorites.

We split up, me going one block left, and Frank one block right. Now we had their car between us—at least, I hoped we did. We both were going as fast as we could, dodging traffic and pedestrians, trying to get ahead of the black sedan.

After a mile or so, I thought it was time to cut back over. I came back out onto Bigelow and looked behind me. There was the sedan, all right, coming straight for me!

I sped ahead of them, but not too far. I could see the sedan coming closer and closer now, clearly trying to run me down. Then Phil leaned out the passenger window and started firing at me!

I swerved from side to side to throw off his aim and wondered where Frank was—until I spotted him just ahead of me, pulling into the traffic on Bigelow.

How had he gone that much faster than me? Well, I had no time to think about that now—the car was almost on me, Phil was still firing away, and Frank wasn't much farther ahead.

This time of night, this stretch of Bigelow Boulevard was empty of both cars and people.

Perfect.

Frank turned back to me and yelled "NOW!!"

I hit the hot button, hard. Instantly, a spray of slippery oil and sharp tacks hit the pavement. I didn't look back, but I could hear the screeching of brakes and tires as the sedan lost control and went into a skid.

I sure hoped no one got hurt, but at that point, it was either Eberhardt and Phil or me and Frank.

I pulled up to the curb and raised my visor. I could see the sedan half a block behind, its hood rammed into a streetlight, smoke rising into the air above it.

"Let's go get 'em!" shouted Frank.

We sped back to the site of the crash and hauled Eberhardt and Phil from the front seats. Both of them were groggy, but they didn't look too bad otherwise. Their air bags had kept them from more serious injury—but nothing was going to keep them from their day in court!

It was a week later, and Frank and I were back at the East Side Mall for the first time since the case wrapped up.

Speaking of wraps, we were chowing down on some Healthy Wraps with Iola, Chet, Adriana, and Steph.

All the stalls were doing a brisk business today— except for Phil's Phranks 'n' Phries, which had a sign saying CLOSED—STORE FOR RENT. Phil and Eberhardt were currently in the Bayport jail, being held without bail as they waited for their trial.

"Wow, these are really good!" Frank said, admiring his wrap.

"I told you," I said. "I was shocked myself, but it's true. They're much better when they're not soaked in plastic."

"When we make the mall over," Steph told us, "everything at the food court is going to be healthy and organic. It's part of the new theme Grandpa and I have come up with—this place is going to be more people-friendly *and* more earth-friendly."

"You really think you can make money that way?" I asked.

"Hey, I don't hear any of you complaining about the wraps," she answered with a smile. "If everything at the food court's this good, we won't have a problem."

Chet nodded enthusiastically, although the words he mumbled were a complete mishmash, due to the mouthful of wrap he was chewing on.

"I think it's great," Adriana said. "I hope there'll still be a job for me here."

"Are you kidding?" said Steph. "You're my store manager from now on—I won't have time to run

In the Groove, since I'll be running the whole operation here."

"Wow, Steph, that's awesome!" Adriana exclaimed.

"Hey, I owe my freedom to you guys," Steph pointed out.

"Well," I said, getting up, "Frank and I have got to go hit the books. We're about a week behind on our homework."

Frank got up too, and we said good-bye to our friends.

"Hey, Frank," I said on our way out, "now that Shangri-La is in bankruptcy, I see a real business opportunity."

"Oh, yeah? What's that?"

"What do you say we go into the mall development business?"

"I think we'd better stick to our day jobs, Joe."

"You mean at the food court?"

"You know what I mean," he said, and gave me a secret wink.

He may be my big brother, but when he's right, he's right.